Dona Nobis Pacem

BEATE SIGRIDDAUGHTER

Part I:

Out In the World

IMAGINE

Imagine you are a goddess in a field of war. You look into the haunted eyes of someone dying, a young man, a beautiful man, dark hair, dark eyes, red blood, vast pain. And his soul begins to sing to you his ache before his vision is eclipsed.

"They were so proud of me when I marched by in uniform. I wanted them to love me. And they did."

His soul is already beyond pain now, puzzled in light, but his mind still carries on with his wishes for anything but the knowledge of burst flesh, with his longing to be allowed to stay for the beauty of a future.

"They were so proud of me for volunteering to die."

Imagine you are a goddess walking a world where we adore each other for something other than sacrifice. Then you would surely sing.

You gently close his eclipsed eyes.

GOOD FRIDAY – MARY MAGDALEN

And many women were there beholding afar off . . .
Matthew 27:55

. . . and, yes, I was with them.

I speak to you from that shimmering distance. The cool of night has lifted. The sun burns into the sand. I speak to you from its hot wind shadows. I speak to you from its dolorous weight. God's son asks for water. I am too far away to hear. They torture him with vinegar.

For two thousand years you have celebrated this day of slaughter. What have you learned?

I speak to you from a time of sorrow and weakness. Women were stoned for making love. Men were crucified for believing in God. What have we learned? And how did we ever learn to diminish, to kill each other so?

My heart hangs twisted between hope and despair. Sacred lives trickle and shift like sand raked by wind. I do not want his sacrifice to be in vain.

"Master," I said, "must there be sacrifice at all?"

He looked up from the sand in which he liked to trace shapes and words. "Beloved, some things in life are worth a sacrifice. Peace is, and love is. Sacrifice is never necessary. Sometimes, though, it is the price exacted."

He could have stirred up rebellion. Many would have fought at his side. His life-blood message was, you do not increase peace or love by fighting.

What does it feel like to watch your beloved prodded in the sun, thirsty, up the gritty hill, in order to be crucified?

Look around. Ask a woman whose husband is sent into action, whose son is sent to the front.

There is a numbness, a distance of disbelief. Death slides between you like a pleading grin that hangs in your faces as you try to reassure one another. The truth is, he just got a one-way ticket to death. He might not return.

You pray on your knees. You know that miracles exist. Riddled with doubt, you keep telling yourself that you believe. You pray so hard, you see stones glitter with pity.

A miracle is something like a simple law of life. If no one nails his hands, his feet, to the cross, if no one raises the cross, then life continues. If no one raises these guns, these swords . . . so possible . . . the hammer not raised, the nail not nailed in.

You keep praying. You make your private deals with God. You remember even men with stones all ready in their hands have laid them down again when fearless words were spoken.

You would give your life if his could be spared that way. But your life is not wanted now. It is not nearly as important as his.

A mad thought grinds in the brains of people with clout, and you are helpless.

What does it feel like to have your loved one nailed to the wood?

I am numb. I am ill. I am so full of hope.

My nerves have forgotten me. I place one foot in front of the other in the sand. This cannot be. This is my friend, my master. He touched. He ate, drank wine. He slept.

I am waiting for the miracle. What will it look like? God's will—I know this—cannot be slaughter. My heart knows this.

Was I his lover? His wife? Does it matter?

It was a man's world then. It is a man's world now. I was a footnote. Yes, and I sat at his feet like a child. I wanted to serve him forever.

And so I got sprinkled into unauthorized texts—a few kisses on the mouth, a special love. Two thousand years later, women are still footnotes in this awkward version of reality—ciphers, trophies, curiosities.

I stepped through the sand, heavy with dread and light with hope, tied to the reluctant muscle of my being. I wanted resolution. Not his death. I wanted to behold the miracle.

I was so convinced that there would be a miracle. I stood with the women, afar off, to watch the miracle take place.

I cannot understand how cruel we can be with one of our own. Never have I heard of lions joking and rolling dice at the foot of the cross of one of their own they have just nailed there to die. Never have I heard of tigers crucifying their males, stoning their females—savoring the spectacle, the agony, the body that keeps twitching with persistent will to live despite the pain, the depletion.

My torment was that I was utterly helpless.

Of course I was in love with him. There was nothing pious about my love, but it was sacred, oh, yes. He was a man with all of God's beauty. How could I not love him, and in him the glory of life?

Such love—any love perhaps—is never deemed significant enough for history.

I loved him.

I would have given him all that I had and anything else he might ask of me, and more—oil, spice, my hair to dry his feet with a caress. He was a prince of peace among the paupers so intent on slaughter.

I stumbled in the sand and fell to my knees. Today the women kneel on cold wood or carved stone—old women often, with kerchiefs on their hair, or respectable hats. They come in their sadness and offer empty, broken, shriveled, yearning lives. They come and believe—he hears them. They dream of a young God righting the unbalanced, toppling world, giving himself, doing what gods do, with reverence for life.

They dream of redemption in this place where they were sent as girls to have a great weight placed upon their life's exuberance, a lid on the bubbles of joy that burst from the effervescence of being. They pray to be given back that beauty of being—alive.

Iraq, Vietnam, Korea, the Philippines, Tokyo, Paris, London, Dresden. A woman trembles in her lover's arms on the eve of his leaving. Later she only trembles with his memory, and with the dread of what it means to have a loved one called up to likely death.

You walk up to Golgotha, one step, then another, with his mother by your side, your eyes on his body, bloody with torture and wretched with humiliation.

Have we bred no end of cruelty into our men? Now they are forced to force themselves upon the beauty of life and make it count for nothing. Nothing is honored until long after death.

The high sun breathes life-giving, but still indifferent power. Everywhere there is a cross, a death. The sand burns the soles of his feet, and mine.

"Master, are you trying to prove that you can live your truth without shedding another man's blood? And can you do that without spilling your own?"

Is death just the ripeness of life tearing open to release its seed?

Am I the one he saved from being stoned to death? It makes a pretty story. I then followed him, a beautiful sinner, saved.

"Woman, where are your accusers?"

No one comes forward to accuse.

What is this preoccupation with sin? When just being alive seems already a sin, to love with touch is certainly unspeakable.

I am in love. I wish I could change his terrible philosophy, his love for this stark father vision of God, for barren laws. I wish I could make him understand that light and life is our gift from God, so much more beautiful than any of us could have dreamed.

But we twist it and twist it and twist it, until it is a hewn length of tree standing up, reeking of blood, pain and fear, and not bearing fruit.

Women often love a man in pain they hope to heal. So many of us stand at a cross, afar off, not daring to come closer.

We offer water with our pitcher when he passes by. We sob. We wipe up the blood with our clothes. We scream in our helpless souls.

"And still, Master, I do not want to stop you from doing what is so important to you."

Here is my staggering dream: I reach the cross before the first nail goes in. I say, "Stop." So simple. Just, "Stop." Reaching out with an unbelievable hand.

Is there a knife in my back for dreaming too much?

In dreams I live in strength and tenderness. Footnotes contain the unwritten. Nothing is spelled out about the women watching from afar.

Yet once we enter the ritual circle of slaughter, we fear the knives in our backs, the stones poised to crush our skulls, our kidneys, our breasts, as though to teach us to practice for death all life long.

But death is easy. Our frailty is its guarantee. Life is what calls for mastery.

It's not as I thought it would be. The sky tears. It is raining.

Among the women in the distance, I am too dizzy with dread to notice the soldiers roll dice for his clothes, or the vinegar sponge.

We shiver with fear and with fever, first in the sun, then in the rain. We do not have the strength left for another step forward to lay a hand on the soldier's arm. We stand and we shiver.

What would it look like a few steps closer?

Perhaps I would not have that knife in my back, but merely provoke a quick, humiliating scuffle.

I struggle, slip, and stumble on the sand. "No. Let me be. Let him be. Let me go to him. He has done nothing to die for."

"Just look at the bitch! She has the hots for him still. Hey, bitch, he can't do it to you any longer. But I'll be happy to."

A soldier grabs my shoulders, rips my black shawl. I spill from torn cloth to the sand. They spit with laughter. If I am lucky, one of the other soldiers stops him, saying, "Cool it, Tertius. Let her be."

The other women shiver and look on with dread and love from afar off.

It's not that God is indifferent. He yearns for our love as much as we yearn for his.\

Look how heavy his sky is with thunder and downpour, how sparkling his sand is in the sun, the dust in his air.

Can you not see that God isn't the one destined to save his son from human hands? This was my loved one's mission, to stop the slaughter by making it visible. If he doesn't succeed, who will?

How much I want to reach for him.

After the death, the women dance their agony. They trample the green wheat of spring. How dare you, God? They sway at the altars, buckling in their knees, their spines. How dare you, God?

But God's laws are simple, you see. Sons are not killed by God's will, but by human bullets, nails, swords, bombs. Husbands, brothers, fathers, neighbors.

You haven't come this far merely to poke in my suffering for jewels.

Why don't you seek my joy instead? Why don't you ever come to seek my joy, the spring blossom pleasure, the quivering lantern of dragonfly wings?

I know the answer of course.

I *am* one of you, twisted, and seduced by death, seduced for thousands of years, by a suffering that compels us to love, to wish that we could heal, allowing wounds, accepting the burden of soothing.

The women, the footnotes, are always funding the truth, some with their broken passions, some with frigidity, and some with money. And all the men seem so in love with pain.

"I wish you could love life enough to stay with us, my lord."

It is not God who forsakes my beloved.

God is as helpless as the women lurking in the distance.

I beg you, women of the future, reach back into my past, give me the courage to step farther still.

God is as powerful and as helpless as the sun. We have to finish the reality. That's the contract we enter when we accept the prize of life.

God, give me the courage for one more step, for speech instead of silence.

Women hang back in the shadow with useless wisdom, huge-eyed like caged monkeys, oblivious to power, which has become a very complicated dance. Wisdom whispers it doesn't have to be this way. Tradition spins, projecting and protecting, moneys, status, things, importance, impotence, and jealousies.

He loves. He is loved. He has the wealth of unbelievable power. Let's cut him down a notch, or two. This is how power will always be stopped. For some, it is the hardest to forgive that someone else can draw from the wellspring of love while they have long forgotten the taste. Money tastes more familiar, doesn't it? The taste of laws and ownership is easy to remember.

Oh, let the law be love. And if it isn't, let it become so.

The miracle is looking at each other, each by each, and starting to obey the simple laws of God. If you do not slaughter your brothers, your sisters, they need not die a violent death. There is no bargaining with this.

And there is this, the toughest law of God: God, too, obeys his own laws. God has no shortcuts. God can only nurture what reality has set in motion. The miracle is in my hands. My hands are tied. Oh, let my hands be unbound.

How far is the glistening arm of the Roman soldier? How much sand between me and his muscle?

God cannot intercede. Remember that.

Ecce homo. He wants to prove that peace is possible. What more could we want? Life is who we are. Life is what we wanted. There is no reason for rage in this world. There is no reason for love in this world. Why then choose rage over love?

Sometimes a restless woman paces far away, as though she smells a possibility beyond the fence of fear. But mostly the women stand still, huge-eyed and helpless.

Even if I am wrong, I must walk with courage.

My body trembled for him in artless desire. If only I could show him the joy of this world, I thought, perhaps he would choose to stay, for my sake, for the sake of celebrating life.

But he was too taken with sorrow for that.

When all our avenues for ecstasy are blocked, then sorrow seeps in, like seeds of depression attaching themselves to our DNA. And suddenly the law is all there is.

And then the law starts growing out of proportion, a powerful vine, choking the heart.

My loved one knew how to heal, how to pick wheat on the Sabbath, how to outwit the pious crowd of men intent on murder who came to test him with a woman who, the law decreed, had to be stoned with stones till she died.

Laws have always circled harsh around women, chaining us to years and tears of silence. You cannot commit adultery alone. But you dare not repeat such thoughts to the inflamed. They only punish you more then. For being a woman, for being wrong, for being their awkward, ever-present temptation. It's faster to kill the temptation than to enlighten the tempted.

Do you wonder that we stand feverish and watch, like sad crows from the distance, skittish like starving cats? We have grown smaller, stunted in the distance, ugly with fear, like monkeys scattering at a clap of hands.

My body was flooded with fear. Also with hope. I didn't want to believe that a decree of men of little consequence would triumph over his power, his life; or that he, like one addicted in his DNA to suffering, should choose the solemn sacrifice over the wild dance and dignity of life.

I, too, am subject to the laws of God.

I didn't believe he would go and let himself get slaughtered. Something, at the last moment, would happen to save him. I knew it. By the time I realized that nothing miraculous was going to take place unless I made it happen, it was too late. I was too weak with disbelief.

I was that miracle, you see, and I was too weak to happen.

We all dream that in the core of our being we can bring the seed of salvation to troubled men we love. We are not wrong.

Of course he was the son of God. Of course you and I are the sons and the daughters of life.

In my attention to grief I became one of the sinners, witness to all this, first flooded with sorrow, then calm with acceptance that we took this life, this God, and shredded him to pieces.

Why did I not step in front of his precious body?

I was so small, confused, befuddled, and I kept believing against reason that it wouldn't happen. In my distance, I even believed in the ability of God to do something so powerful that my beloved wouldn't die, to act like a parent who has the magic to fix what we have broken.

Well, your church masters say triumphantly, he didn't die, did he? He is still with us.

Only, he was never human again. We believe in a savior who will not be human again. Do we then also believe in a salvation that will never be human again?

Ask the women with men at war how they pray, what miracles they beg for, how they believe their men will return, against all odds, and in the face of all reality.

I knew from the first I would be wounded by loving him, and by his love for a jealous God who excluded all else, especially all things of earth. Should he, in the desert, have chosen the green earth that Satan offered him, rather than the elusive love of God?

True God is not jealous. True God is not at war with angels.

I could feel both his passion and his errors. That was perhaps my greatest sin: to know his errors and not speak of them, for fear of embarrassing him, for fear of stopping the passion together with the mistake.

I also felt his blessing ways. Each moment in his presence was a gift. Keeping respectful silence seemed a small price to pay. And yet it was too great.

When he was dead, yes, I went to the cross to touch, too late, the lifeless feet, the blood-crusted flesh. The flies sipped the last bit of life from his blood, which smelled metallic in coagulation. I remember the stench of fear. And still I kissed his stained feet. Behold, this is my beloved.

The diamond grains of sand ground into my knees, into the palms of my hands.

Did I rage against God?

No, God raged against me.

When my loved one cried out on the cross, did he realize at last that he had prayed at the wrong altar? It was not God he should have prayed to, but the men, the hearts of the men that had condemned him from senseless envy, the ones who were his equals, the ones who could have turned the tide.

And he should have prayed to the women who were on his side all along because they were on the side of love and of life all along . . . but so far off in their fears.

You seem to care a lot whether we lay together in love. Is that so important?

I wanted nothing so much as to touch him, to love my lord. The love was important, not how he chose to receive it.

I wanted to kiss him, even his lifeless flesh.

I didn't want him to be gone. I did not want to be apart from him.

Sadder than all is that, near two thousand years later, not much has been learned.

Be gentle with each other.

Don't weep with me or for me today. Rather, reach back in time and give me the courage I need to step out of the shadows and put my hand on the Roman soldier's arm. And pray for me to reach forward in time to give you the courage for a future of peace.

Pray with me at the foot of the cross of my lord. Pray that we may not just receive the blessings of his teaching like children do, but that we may also start to grow with them, as adults, as God's sons and God's daughters, strong against the sin of silence.

Pray to step forward from among the women watching from afar, who have been ridiculed, who have been trivialized, who have been humiliated, and yet, who still go forth and celebrate the beauty of life.

This is where the tears fade, the smudges, the odor of fear, the slime of carnage. This is the truth of a woman who wanted to love and be loved. To live. To protect.

You've seen me, red-cloaked at times in your salacious fantasies, kneeling in despair, in tragedy, in sorrow. Don't look there anymore. Look where my love for him was tenderness. I wanted to sit in the curl of his arm. I wanted to sit beside him and worship, for he taught me everything that he believed.

The walk was long up to the cross.

I am on my knees in the sand. If there is heckling, I can't hear it. I only dream of standing up, of claiming my desire.

Come closer. I would offer you the future. Your hand on the soldier's arm. Your word pregnant with power.

"Stop."

ONE YEAR

I should have started sooner writing this down. There's so little time now. I want to hold on to everything. I don't want things to change. Again. But they will. Maybe there will be an extra day if a train goes off schedule. Not likely. Before I know it, Monika will be here to pick me up. Then I'll once again be the respectable widow, mother of three, old lady, good citizen.

I want to hold on to the freedom of this last year.

I don't really want to go back to tedious respectability. But I will.

Okay, no time to waste. Only just enough time to look up at the sliver moon through the window. Soon it will fade into day.

The moon was full when I arrived. Good thing, because I didn't even have a flashlight. Matches in a tin canister, yes, but they don't do much good outside. I had a stump of a candle, too. But I'm no pilgrim marching along with a lit candle in hand, the way we used to march as children in the first week of advent with our cardboard lanterns. I do like the idea, though: Pilgrim Mina.

I can't remember if it was windy the night I got here. Probably not, otherwise I would remember the pleasure of finding shelter.

I had said goodbye to Amelia. I had to. She didn't want us to split up. True, it would have been safer to keep on traveling together. She even invited me to come live with her at her cousin's home in a place called Waldsee. She offered to share her room with me until I found my own family again. Unfortunately, she was driving me crazy.

I said I'd stay in touch, but I didn't. By then she probably was offended anyway. No matter what polite justifications I thought up, I'm sure she could sense I was simply fed up with her company.

In my defense, I stayed with her until she had only a day's journey left to get to her cousin's. It wasn't as though I abandoned her in the wild somewhere. And there was that other group she joined in the end. Yes, it would have been safer, and, yes, I lied, telling her and everyone else that I had a lead on finding some of my family up north. I didn't. In fact, what lead I had was that Marianne and the kids were heading to Bavaria when they left my house. I went in the opposite direction on purpose, heading north.

I'd already lost everything, my house, my workshop. My family was gone to destinations as yet unknown. The one thing I wanted to hold on to was my little bit of autonomy—not an easy prospect in our world, war or no war.

I suppose you could say I went crazy. The hunger. A sixty-one-year-old woman wandering on country roads with her small bundle, sleeping on haystacks, hiding in trees. Truth? I was gleefully proud to still be able to climb up a tree. Most women my age were too large or lately too weak to climb anything.

It was just my knapsack and me. Yes, you could say I was crazy. I didn't feel crazy, though. Despite the hunger and the grime, I felt delicious. The air was mine. I had room to expand in it. I didn't have to constrict myself around it. For the first time in my life, I was truly free.

Hunger is a mean thing, though. It gnaws at you. It was too early for ripe grain. I tried. There were kernels already. They tasted liquid and green. At times I ate them anyway. Once I passed through a town where everybody stood in line for a tablespoon of sugar. I didn't want sugar. I wanted bread. But the English doled out sugar, so I took sugar. And in the fields the unripe grain. I remember I got some milk a few times, too. Milk always made me happy. Skim milk tasting of miracles.

Once I ate fresh bread until the hiccups came. I didn't care. The bread in my mouth felt wonderful.

I found a man on the road. At first I thought he was sleeping, but he was dead. I went through his knapsack and found several tins of Kommissbrot and a roll of dried pea soup. I took them. I left him there. I had to trust that someone else would find and bury him. It wasn't something I could do all by myself. I was afraid he would haunt me for leaving him there, but the only time I ever think of him, I feel gratitude, as though he were telling me: You did well.

I didn't know where to go, so I just went.

I hoped the children were okay, and my three little grandchildren, but I didn't give them a lot of thought. I had no desire to go find them. Strange, isn't it? I deliberately went in the other direction.

It was beautiful for the first days alone on the road. Nobody bothered me. Then came a few days of rain. It wasn't too bad. It was still summer. I sat under trees to wait out the rain. I wasn't afraid of lightning. I figured if the Lord had saved me this far, He wouldn't let me die from a bolt of lightning unless He had a good reason.

And then I saw Gerhard's farm. I was wet. I watched the farmhouse for a while. No sign of life. So I went to the barn.

I didn't care for anything anymore. By then my favorite time of day was whenever I was exhausted enough to fall asleep.

I was delirious.

He brought me beef broth.

I apparently babbled in my delirium and called out for Erich.

"Gerhard," he told me he kept saying, assuming I had misunderstood him the first time. "My name is Gerhard."

"But where is Erich?" I asked.

"Who is Erich?"

"My husband of course." How could he be so dense?

Potatoes. He had potatoes in the cellar, with eyes sprouting, but they were okay. We could eat them, boiled, fried, turned into potato dumplings, potato pancakes. Even potato cake.

The first thing he got was chickens.

Then a cow.

I had nothing to give him.

When Tillmann's wife left my house, she forgot to take the six tins of Kommissbrot Tillman had brought as a gift for her the winter before. They were still good. They were supposed to last forever.

I told him my name. Wilhelmina Weber.

"Are you a weaver?" Gerhard asked.

"No, but close. I'm a dressmaker. Perhaps I should say I was a dressmaker. There's not going to be a lot of demand for new dresses in the near future."

"You never know," he said.

He came down from the attic with curtain materials. "There," he said. "Sew something." I appreciated his gentle generosity. He knew I didn't want to be just a charity case.

While I was on the road, I never slept in trees. I slept in haystacks at times, though, like a cat. With the trees, though I could climb them, I was afraid I would fall out, never mind all the fairy tales I had read with grandmother witches sitting up in trees. Nobody ever mentioned any of them actually sleeping in those trees. As for me, I was sure I would fall out.

Gerhard had a rickety motorcycle. One day he came with a huge jar of pickled herring.

He always told me I ate too little. Half a slice of bread with butter and a leaf of lettuce. Bread and butter. Bread with sugar. With goose drippings or pork drippings. One of my favorites was milk rice when we had milk.

I am paralyzed. I am frantic. I wanted to write down everything all at once. All that freedom this past year. I want to keep every morsel of it alive.

When Marianne left with the children, I should have gone too, but I didn't want to. I didn't have a lot of use for Marianne. I thought she was a silly little thing. I don't know what possessed Tillmann to bring her to me in the middle of a war. I guess for her and the children's safety. I guess he knew I wouldn't abandon her or kick her out. She should have stayed with her own parents, but I didn't have a way of saying so without sounding mean. She didn't have a trade. Nothing. Her cooking was marginal, too. I'm just saying—

what good was she then? She once wanted to be a teacher. Would probably have done okay with that, come to think of it, but her father had said no. I am grateful my father let me learn his trade. I am grateful I had at least something useful to offer the world.

But here was little Marianne. The year she lived with me she played the piano a lot. When I had customers, too. Though there weren't a lot of those left. In times of war, in a town as small as ours, a glorified village, who had the ambition to order a new wardrobe? I did a lot of mending. Especially coats and uniforms. Mending didn't mean I had to know much about men's tailoring. I just had to fix what was already there. Marianne could have done that too, but she claimed she didn't have the skills. To prove it, she'd regularly stick her needle into her finger and get blood on something. Creative ineptitude.

She'd tell me people said it gave my dressmaker shop class to have someone play the piano in the background. I'm sure that's what people would say to her to her face. Behind our backs, I expect they were wondering what windfall we had just had to be able to afford a piano. She'd brought it from her parents' home up in East Prussia, of course. At some expense, too, because last I checked, pianos don't walk.

Anyhow, when she left I still thought I could hold on to everything I owned. After all, I was no longer young. Nobody was going to be enticed to rape me, I thought. I was old and scrawny. And murder? They'd murder me in Bavaria or Hannover as likely as they'd murder me back home. Where I at least had my house.

Then of course no sooner had they left—I think it was less than a month—things went downhill. She had traveled off in the cattle car with her three little ones. The youngest was only born at the end of December. I thought at a month and a half, or just short of two months, the little one was too weak to travel. But Marianne wouldn't leave her behind with me. I don't blame her. And of course war and disaster don't happen at our convenience. She was right to get out when she could. Less than a month later, we lost our town to Polish troops, then regained it for three days, and then it was taken again. For good this time.

At first it looked like we could stay. I didn't really care under what government I lived, so long as I could just go about my business. But then it became uncomfortable. There were Russians in the mix, too, now, and we heard terrible things. In May, when Germany surrendered, there were rumors of Russians raping and pillaging wherever they went. I still thought I was too old and scrawny to tempt anyone to rape me. Then fear kept growing louder anyhow.

Suddenly I no longer officially owned my house. I had squeezed myself into a little room in the attic. I was afraid to go down to the kitchen. I couldn't speak more than a few words of Polish. That's where Marianne would have been of some use because she grew up on a farm with Polish workers, and she knew to make herself understood. But she was long gone by now. Hale and safe with her three babies, I hoped.

The discomfort kept growing. The dream of staying in my own place simply died.

How difficult could it be, I thought, to get to Bavaria and find Marianne? Monika was further west in Baden-Württemberg and Gabi was somewhere else, I had no idea where. There were no trains in the middle of 1945 anymore—not for civilians anyhow. But one could still walk. I was strong. I was convinced I was still capable of wandering.

Tillmann had once gone on a wandering tour with a friend, just before the war broke out when there was widespread unemployment and neither Tillmann nor his friend could find work. Or rather, work, yes, but no pay. For half a year's work, Tillmann once finally got a kitchen cabinet. Not something we needed. Anyway, the wandering was Goethe-inspired. Working his way as a journeyman through the country while seeing something of the world. I decided if my son could do it, then I could do it too. True, I was not a youngster. True, I was a woman. "Only" a woman, as I had heard far too often in my long life.

I packed a bundle.

Of my three children, I miss my beautiful Gabi most of all, and she's probably the one who could care about me the least. Monika—I don't know. Tillmann is now with his Marianne and the kids.

My current situation is familiar. I'd prefer staying here and keeping my distance. I don't want what is happening. First Monika's letter. She had found me. I felt guilty. She found out that I was still alive, and I hadn't been desperately looking for them. Then the telegram from Monika that she's arriving next Friday. I knew it was coming of course. I wish it were Gabi instead of dour Monika. But Monika is the dutiful one.

It's as though my life doesn't belong to me. And it doesn't, does it?

The Leitners now always invite me to go to church with them and share their Sunday dinner afterwards. I don't want to do either. I suppose if I were pious, it would be easier. But

I'm not. If God had wanted me to believe in Him, He would have given me the requisite pious disposition.

The real killer here is, the Leitners don't really want me at their family dinner. They feel they have to invite me, poor lonely old widow that I am. Then I feel that I cannot in all conscience say no to their unwanted graciousness. They'd rather relax among themselves. And I'd rather be in my own room with a piece of bread. But I don't have a good excuse. I have noticed this all my life. People allow the following excuses: work commitments and prior commitments to other people. That's it. Personal preference for solitude doesn't count. Other than the aforementioned acceptable excuses, they feel free to involve you in their activities because you have, after all, nothing else to do.

I loved it when the kids were small. They were my very acceptable excuse to get out of any and all extraneous commitments. Kids trump everything, even God. Kids or illness. But in the case of kids, then they are there, underfoot, with their ten thousand needs. And illness I can do without.

Sometimes I wish I had Monika's faith in God. She's been steadfast, even when Hitler and his men made it unfashionable to be a churchgoing Christian. She clung to her church and her good works. She's tried to make me a believer as well. It isn't happening. I am curious about her belief. Is it genuine? Or is it something she has latched onto, like Tillmann once latched onto undying loyalty to the Fatherland?

I wish I had a badge to wear like they do—a badge of loyalty or devotion to something.

I'm worried about Tillmann—now that the Fatherland is in ruins and surrendered, where will he put his allegiance?

What will give him meaning? Maybe Monika will persuade him into the ranks of followers of her Lord Jesus. I think he needs someone, something to follow. I'm glad I made him learn his carpentry trade. People will always need furniture. I know he wanted to be a teacher. And so we both missed out. I, too, would have loved to have been a teacher. And then his wife, his Marianne. Odd, how we all wanted to be teachers and none of us are. I'm a middling dressmaker, currently making curtains for Gerhard. Tillman is an unemployed soldier/carpenter, and Marianne is a housewife without a house. Monika writes they live with a farmer in a small village in Bavaria.

Gabi, she might go on to be the successful one in our family. She's the one who actually studied to become a teacher—the third child, the lucky one in any self-respecting fairy tale. I wonder if she's still being courted by all these men. She's the independent one. I wonder what I did right to make her who she is. I wonder what we can do to keep her that way. I so wish it was she and not Monika coming to get me.

I'll probably not find out much about her because she and Monika haven't exactly seen eye to eye over the years. I wonder how much it has cost Gabi spiritually to resist all efforts to avoid the allure of the herd.

I fear I'll end up with two spinster daughters. Monika is too pious and docile to attract anyone, and Gabi is too independent and feisty. I want to protect Gabi. It's not that she's not attractive, but she's already said no so many times. Among her suitors were one count and one professor of history. I ought to want to protect Monika, really. She's the one who has to make it through this life on a crutch of piety.

But I can't stand her piousness. Gabi is more like a colorful bird or some huge flamboyant flower.

But never mind my brave Gabi. I need to prepare myself and be brave for my own rather less promising future. Everybody assumes that Monika is not only coming to visit me but will also take me to live with her. What can I possibly say to her?

I've been hiding out here, and I have been found, and I will have to get ready for my next prison term in polite and respectable society.

Should I feel guilty that I have used the cruel post-war times to eke out a little slice of autonomy for myself?

I don't understand our society. Or why we have to strangle each other to make each other fit for polite society. I want to be wild. I will be tame.

I've wanted to be in love all my life, and I've avoided love like the plague after Erich. In case I would sully Erich's memory. Gerhard would have been a good one to love.

Gerhard.

I remember.

I had just gone through four days of rain, then dry, then rain again. I was exhausted. I'd seen farms, but no towns, and every time I thought I'd get to some farm house and ask for some milk, and offer to work for food and shelter, I'd decide to move on instead at the last minute.

The one time I had stopped, on the second day of rain, I was dripping wet. The farm woman opened the door, looking nice and remarkably fat for these times, and I could smell some kind of meat cooking. I asked for milk and a piece of bread or a potato if she could spare it. And could I help around the farm for a place to sleep in the stables for the night?

"Help?" she sized me up as though I had just asked the most ridiculous question. I guess I looked wet and scrawny and not exactly young.

"I'll give you a glass of milk and a hunk of break," she said. "But you'll have to drink the milk outside. Leave the glass over there." She pointed to a small walled area that included a wooden A-frame doghouse. "And then I don't want to see you again."

"I have a cup," I said, reaching for my knapsack.

"You'll take my glass," she insisted.

"Thank you," I said when she handed me the milk and the bread. I went to sit on the wall surrounding the doghouse. I looked at the dog's dish that had boiled grain in it and a bone with some cooked meat still on it. How envious I was. It was a handsome German shepherd with a healthy-looking coat of hair. I envied him his shelter, his coat, his food. It's probably my imagination, but I thought he pushed over his meaty bone in my direction.

"No thanks," I whispered. "I'm not quite there yet." Meaning eating meat off a dog's bone. It probably had some lovely marrow in it, too.

I looked into the dog's eyes and they looked kind and full of sorrow. I guess most dogs' eyes do. It's either that or begging. This one didn't even seem to consider hinting about my piece of bread.

Maybe I took too long looking into the dog's eyes. "You have to move on now," I heard the woman's voice behind me. I can't blame her. Everything was in turmoil. Everyone was suspicious.

For the next two days I spoke to no one. I ate some unripe peaches from a tree and some unripe grain, and I drank water from a brook. I looked in birds' nests, but they were all empty. I'd have to catch something.

I still had one tin of Kommissbrot left. I didn't want to open it. I wanted to save it as a last resort because once I ate it, then what? Hunger alone isn't so bad. It's when it's flavored with fear that it becomes terrible. Will I ever eat enough again in my life?

You have a lot of time to think and fear when you wander through a beautiful landscape that is marred by defeat, suspicion, and destruction. I considered stealing a chicken somewhere, like a fox, but I hadn't seen a chicken for days. Probably they were all in someone's soup or else carefully locked away to lay eggs. I'd never understood how hens could lay egg after egg with no noticeable periods of rest. Sounds unnatural to me. I mean blackbirds and robins have a season or two for laying eggs. The end.

Then again, I'll never understand how human beings can have sex without a season—over and over and over again. Okay, I don't want to dwell on that just now.

But of course that's what's on my mind. I thought for a while it would be better next time to try my luck with a male farmer—who would possibly be more friendly. Hard times and all, most men were still raised to be more or less chivalrous. But what if they weren't? There was always the possibility I'd have to pay with my body, and then they might just laugh at me and I'd have paid in vain, be told to move on anyway.

So far I'd avoided rape and prostitution.

I remember Amelia saying she'd not be unreasonably proud. "It's just sex and I want to live." It makes me nauseated just to think about selling my body.

And yet, what an easy inbuilt way to get something one needs. Food. Shelter. Protection.

I knew it was possible. Even for an old woman like myself. Someone told me when men get in the mood, the woman in front of them, any woman, becomes beautiful on the spot. Never having been a man, I wouldn't know. It would be easy for me. I can no longer get pregnant. And I may be scrawny, but I'm not ugly.

"But I don't want that," I thought in those days. "Not yet. I'm not that desperate yet. Maybe one day, if there is no other way. The same day I'd eat meat from a dog's bone."

I'd heard of people eating dogs and rats. And horse meat, of course. I think I've had that—though it was advertised as beef when I had it. It tasted sweeter than usual. In any event, when you're desperate, you don't ask too many questions.

A rabbit. Maybe one day I'd eat a rabbit if I could catch one and could make a fire and roast it. But how would I skin it? My pocketknife did not look adequate.

I came to a farm that looked abandoned. The fields weren't tended or orderly. Maybe if I was lucky I'd find a disorderly vegetable or two. A carrot. A cabbage. A radish, a potato.

There was a barn and I opened the door. It smelled of old straw. Not dirty, but not fresh. Like dry leaves on a forest trail in fall. To me the smell was promising. It meant no animals were about—not farm animals, anyway. Incidental critters were sure to be there. Mice. Spiders.

It was dry. It was clean. And I was tired. A mild warmth radiated out from the straw, like the warmth from a dung heap, but minus the dung. And I was so tired.

I'd taken two unripe apples from a tree outside. It was still a struggle to get down unripe fruit. My stomach rebelled against the sourness, but my hunger was huge. I decided to open my last tin of Kommissbrot. But first I would take a nap. No matter that it was the middle of the day. So I curled up in the straw and slept. I must have slept several hours. The sun was still up outside when I woke up. After all, it was summer. But shadows started falling in, and since I was inside, it was getting dark around me.

I had watched the farmhouse for half an hour or so to see if there was any activity before I went in the barn. I didn't want a run-in with anyone. It had appeared totally quiet. No people, no animals. Not even bird activity. So why hadn't I gone into the farmhouse itself? I felt as a person passing through, a refugee, a vagrant, really, I didn't deserve better than a barn. Which I didn't technically deserve either, of course, but it felt like a lesser theft to sleep on straw in someone's abandoned wooden barn than it would have in someone's abandoned stone house. Maybe if it had been in ruins. If I had to "steal" something that wasn't mine and that I would not be able to repay, then it seemed best to take the least valuable thing possible.

I felt the now familiar ache when I woke up, my bones curled up, no great softness underneath, though the straw was as soft as anything I had slept on in days.

I had gotten used to the smell of old straw. There were hay boxes too, along one side of the barn wall, though there were no stall divisions. The boxes themselves were empty, except for a few straggling lengths of dry grass. I looked at some old seemingly intact bales of hay in one corner. I fantasized. Wouldn't it be great to be a horse? Then all I would have to do was eat the hay. Strange that those huge animals were able to digest those puny dried bits of grass and be well-nourished. Why couldn't I? Well, maybe that would be next. For now I would eat my last tin of bread, open it at least and take one or two slices. There would be six slices in all. One would be enough for today, I decided.

One day I will give these reflections to Gabi. I think she, of all my children, would understand best. Last I knew she was working for a bookseller in Heilbronn. But with the war I doubt books are in demand. I do not know.

A gift from heaven! I got up this morning and Frau Leitner says they're not going to church today. Her littlest one fell ill and they have to go to town and will eat their Sunday dinner there. I am so happy. It is indescribable. I will have an extra Sunday to myself, my last Sunday of liberty.

I don't know how I can be so small-minded about this, so protective of my solitude, but I am.

They offered to drop me at church on the way to town, and I said I would walk instead.

What is so strange is that I really like them but sitting through a meal with them is still a burden. Having to behave and to listen to polite small talk. I started walking in the direction of the church, then decided to go for a long walk instead, looking at the trees, making the forest my church. I am so lucky, I am sheltered, fed. Last year this time everything was chaotic, in flux, no knowing what the future would hold, or even if I would live. And here I am alive. I should be so thankful. I *am* thankful. But I am also filled with dread. I can feel it in my stomach like knots. I will have to become respectable again, responsible, accountable, and I don't know how without losing myself. Again. To the dictates of the world.

Why was I not made like other women, happy to be in my place in the world into which I was born? They all seem so content. Are they? Or are they like me, but they cannot say so?

I loved my father. He decided as his only child I was entitled to become his heir, his successor, and so I was entitled to help him and to learn his trade. I know my mother wasn't keen on the idea, but when I was fourteen, I was allowed to become his apprentice. It was delicious. I gladly gave up my school stuff, though I loved to read. I would climb up into the apple tree and sit there and read for hours. When I started my apprenticeship, mother declared that I would still have to do all my household chores and learn to be a useful housewife as well. That, in her opinion, was my real destiny and trade, and if I had ambitions to do something else as well, that would have to be done on the side. She needed my help around the house, now that I was old enough and clever enough to do something. So, in addition to being my father's apprentice, I would clean, cook, and otherwise do whatever was necessary. Mother was stern, but frail. Now that I was old enough to be in charge of the household, she started to relax a bit. It worked well for her. In the end she outlived my vigorous father. At the time, father indulged her. "Well," he'd say to me, "you'll simply have to do both, your work and your work." He'd smile at me and wink. "Your sewing is better than your cooking," he said. "But we'll survive on your food."

Of course being his apprentice, I didn't have to pay for my apprenticeship. So that was a selling point with my mother. Who had, incidentally, done a lot of ancillary work in the dressmaker shop, just not the trade itself.

Anyway, my school days were over, my sitting up in trees and reading was over. With my new responsibilities, there just wasn't time. I was now apprentice dressmaker and apprentice housewife, and I gladly gave up my reading in the apple tree except on Sundays for a little while—after church and again after the Sunday dinner was made, consumed, and cleaned up. I learned poems by heart so I could repeat them to myself throughout the week when I was busy doing other things.

I was happy. I felt useful. And hopeful. I was going to have a beautiful life making clothes for beautiful women and I would be able to put bread and meals on my table, and it is true, it was a blessed thing, for eventually that was my job as a widow with three children.

I liked Erich. It wasn't a great passion, nothing like what I read (and sometimes yearned for) in books, but it was good.

I bless the time I have had to deal only with myself. My place in this world. It seems odd, with the world falling apart around me, the country in surrender. All these visions of horror all about me. The Leitners said over in town three men were hanged once in the town square. Why? They were Germans hanged by Germans. We are our own enemies in this world. Has it always been like that?

And then why am I alive?

I am happy to be alive. What fate has allowed me to still be here?

My girls are here. Both of them. A complete surprise. When the Leitners took me to town to meet Monika's train, it wasn't just Monika, but Gabi as well. I am ecstatic. It gives me this delicious feeling of joy in my chest. I always thought Gabi was not very fond of me. Then she stepped down from the train with her amazing smile.

"You too? Oh, what a wonderful surprise."

"Well, what did you think?" she said while I was trying to keep tears to myself. "Of course I'd come."

I don't know why. Has she forgiven me? I guess there is really nothing to forgive. I was just a stern mother. I am so happy. It is the best thing about this sudden change that is to take place. Seeing her step down from the train, her eyes shimmering, and her words, "Of course I'd come."

Somehow I feel lighter around her.

Why am I so reluctant to be among people? That's easy. They imprison me in this deplorable role of old widow. There are certain rules for old women in this country, and there are certain rules for mothers, and there are certain rules for widows. All of them are strict separately, but if you put them all together, it makes it hard to so much as move or breathe.

What would I do with my life if I were capable of moving freely? I have no idea now. I feel defeated. If I had Gabi's youth and energy, oh, I would soar.

Erich. He was kind and gentle. Without him, I've always been a bit lost, like a roof without walls to hold it up. There were days when I just wanted to be done with it all. I couldn't put the world to rights. So what was the point? There was so much evil. Even now I can't get rid of the idea of men hanging one another or shooting each other in the back for surrendering. Why?

Of course all war is really killing off one another without remorse. It is an anger that has eaten into our souls. My soul is angry, too.

I will tell Gabi how happy she makes me with her strength, her rebellion, all of that. But I can't really. Would she understand if I told her? Or would she think I was the weirdest mother in the world? Mothers don't talk to their children about stuff like that.

Gerhard's wife. I will never get to meet her now. Probably for the best. Very likely I'd despise her for not being with him, for being aloof, and therefore in my book not good enough for him.

After Erich died—1916, my God, that's thirty years ago—I've now been alone for thirty years more or less. Twenty-nine and a bit, but of course he wasn't home much that last year. Gabi is my last connection to him, so no wonder I feel so much for her.

Darklight. That's the only word I am capable of thinking of right now.

We could all be so beautiful.

We are in fact so beautiful. But we are so dreadfully misguided.

We don't have the nerve to be honest with each other, and yet when we are less than honest, we do not live. Not genuinely. And when we are not living genuinely, then it all becomes a burden.

What do we want from each other? Love, I think.

And what do we give each other? Jealousy. Greed. Misery. War.

I can't get the three young men out of my mind. The war was already over. Germany had surrendered. I imagine them young, happy to no longer have to fight a war they barely understood, only that they must be in it. What their horror must have been to realize that their own were now turned against them in a rage for having lost the war. The ones they had fought for and fought with were now the enemy because a good German never surrenders, and a bad German shouldn't be allowed to live.

We are the enemy.

I wonder what it would be like to have no need for escape, to just be gloriously alive and beautiful with all our feelings.

What did I want from life? I wanted a simple life side by side with Erich, making fancy clothes for people richer than we were, and simple clothes for people like us.

I want to praise the world, it is beautiful. I cannot help but admire it, the grasses, the flowers, the trees, the many beautiful things.

I remember the day Gerhard brought me a tin of Schoka-ko-la he had, and we each broke off one segment of the dark chocolate for several days until it was all gone.

I remember how he said one day: "I know we have a book somewhere." Then, after rummaging in his storeroom, he came up with a volume of Goethe poems. I started reciting the one about the violet. So he teased me. "Oh, okay, you don't really need it."

"No, give it to me, give it to me," I said passionately, then added: "If you would, please."

"I liked that flare of passion," he said.

I turned beet red.

So I am sad now. There is nothing to escape to, only myself, over and over, and I am not intrinsically boring, but I am boring when I do not have a true connection with the world.

I wanted to live side by side with Erich all my life. I wanted him to love me fairy tale fashion, and I do think he loved me. But who will ever know?

We were already becoming old hat to each other. Women were interested in him, never mind that he was married to me. Never mind that they were married to other men. That's another thing I find hard to understand. I'd been taught fidelity and love for a lifetime. Not necessarily by my parents' example, but by the fairy tales I read. And of course by my own body's yearning. But apparently that wasn't so for everyone.

It is difficult for me to understand why we do not live with one another in complete awe.

Perhaps the most honest time I have ever lived was when I was hungry on the road last year and still loved the beauty of everything. Sunrise, blades of grass with drops of morning dew. Poppy flowers unfolding their wrinkled dresses, more beautiful than anything I could possibly sew, even if I had the most delicate material.

I want to be important. Other people are always important, but when I am alone, and only when I am alone, I am important, too.

I wonder whether we will have another turnip winter. I wonder if the children remember. They were so young in

1916 and 1917 when we were all so hungry. I was fortunate. I always managed to get bread for all of us somehow.

I don't much like reality. War is the absurdest thing we can do in this world. There's not much I can do about it. I feel so small.

I walked outside most of the day yesterday, appreciating the beauty of this world that has been saved for me and that I am now about to lose again.

How will I explain to the children why I didn't come looking for them? Will it be possible to avoid the subject? I think just maybe I'll be able to pull it off. I'll look extra stern every time anyone broaches the subject, and with any luck they will politely back off.

The Leitners, I'm sure, had something to do with them finding me, trying to do me a favor. And I guess it is a favor.

I am afraid there's nothing left for me to do here. I tried to do my usual house chores earlier today, but Mrs. Leitner waved me off. "I'm sure you have a lot to do."

They assume I will take off with my daughters. And I assume I will, too. Perhaps that's my problem. I'm trapped in a world in which everybody assumes they know what is best and appropriate for me. Nobody asks what I want. Why, that would be preposterous. Ask an old lady what she wants when the path is so clearly marked and prescribed?

Little Katrin is still sick, so I gave her my brocade vest as a gift. She's the only one who will even fit into it and I never wear it. It's the one unnecessary thing I brought with me. It seemed so important to keep one item of beauty. Now I've given it to little Katrin, and she loves it.

She loves me, too, that's the amazing part. I am so happy when children take to me, little children who aren't yet indoctrinated in the ways of being distant and polite in this world. I am so glad when a child loves me. Once Gabi loved me like that.

I am glad that Katrin has my vest, even if she, too, never has any good use for it. I wore it secretly from time to time when I still lived at Gerhard's place, but then he surprised me in it one day. He complimented me profusely, and he was right, it did look special, and I in it. But after his compliments I was too shy to ever wear it again. Funny, too, I didn't realize until I gave my favorite useless garment to a child just how small I am.

It wasn't that I didn't want to see my children again ever, no. It was just that I put off looking for them. I am lost in my own world, and I like it here. I liked it, I should say. Past tense. It is coming to an end. One year. I have never been so alone in all my life, and I have never been so happy.

Gerhard. I remember I was about to lie down in the straw again when his face appeared in the one window of the barn. I could feel all my limbs become numb. My whole life has been lived with a background of fear of men. A terrible, dull fear all the time. And now his face at the window.

When Erich didn't come back from the war in 1916, my parents were still alive. They were willing to take care of me, and I kept working in father's shop as though nothing had happened. After a few years, they wondered why I didn't remarry. Everybody wondered. I simply didn't want to.

The winter of 1916 was hard. No word yet about Erich, though that in itself was ominous. He used to write letters regularly. Then nothing. Then one day the news. Erich was dead.

Children clung to their parents. I don't want to remember. But I have remembered every day of my life.

When he left last, for France, in the summer of 1916, he said, "If I have to die, so long as I know that you and the children are safe here, I will die happy."

I was so young then still. I simply didn't want to admit that he was gone. It was so pointless.

That's one of the reasons perhaps that I didn't want to go find my children. They're grown up. If I didn't know for sure, then I could imagine they were alive and happy somewhere. I didn't want to be looking for them and find that they, too, were gone. Or sick. Or suffering. How often can you lose things in life and still not go insane?

So Gerhard found me in the barn. He was prosaic.

"It would be more comfortable for you over in the house," he said.

"But it's not mine," I said. "I'm only passing through. Do you know who owns it?"

"Yes. I own it," he said. "And you can stay as long as you like. You look like you could use a rest."

The next thing I knew, I was very ill. I want to tell myself that, had he not been there, I would have mustered the strength to carry on, but this little bit of solicitude took the wind out of my sails and out of my soul. I fell apart.

He brought me beef stock he cooked himself.

He washed me.

"I needed to," he said. "You were filthy. You had a high fever. You were lucky, though. You didn't have lice. And I wanted to do something useful in the world."

He brought a chicken and made it into a meal as well. I tried to eat as little as possible, but he still managed to feed me most of it.

"Never you mind how I got that," he said.

He was always cheerful and kind. It has always been hard for me to accept anything from anyone. And he managed to make it easy.

"How can I make good on all of this?" I asked.

"It is good already. We are alive."

He never asked questions, but he made it clear that it was good to tell him things. He reminded me of Alyosha in *The Brothers Karamazov*. That kind of feeling, though I hadn't read the book in a long while, maybe in my early twenties when I was with Erich who was not interested in reading much.

I told him why I didn't want to look for my children. I emphasized the fear, of course, not the weariness of my tiresome role as mother.

He told me I didn't have to do anything I didn't want to do. It would be easier if I declared my presence and registered because then we could both collect food rations. But if I didn't want to, then we would live on his. The end. He was so kind.

We sat side by side one evening watching the sun set, as we often did while I was recovering.

"I'm married, you know," he said. I wanted to laugh out loud. And his point was?

I wish I were back in the early days with Gerhard. He sat on his haunches in front of me in his barn and persuaded me that it would be better for me to stay in a room in the house, at least for a night.

"Pretty clean," he promised. "No spiders. No daddy longlegs."

"I've kind of made my peace with crawly things these last few weeks," I told him.

"Yeah, I suppose you have. How long have you been on the road?"

"Five weeks," I told him.

"All on your own?"

"Just the last two weeks," I said. "Before I was with another woman, and some other people from time to time."

So he persuaded me to go over to the main house with him. I wanted to ask him so many questions. Was it going to be a nuisance to have me there? Was I going to be a burden? That's been my greatest fear all my life—to be a burden, and of course I had to always live my greatest fear. A widow with three children in a country recovering from one war only to stride into the next, what could I be but a burden? True, I was working, I was producing something. It never felt like it was enough.

Anyway, he opened the door to the neatest, prettiest room with white walls and a crucifix over the small bed by the window. The bedding looked so thick and inviting.

"Thank you," I apparently managed to say before I plain fainted away in the middle of the doorway. I don't remember at all, but of course he told me later. He carried me and my meager belongings into the room, then decided to give me that bath. I was mortified when he told me later about the bath. He tried to make light of it. How he wasn't going to put me into that clean bed without me having a bath first. Lice were always a consideration and while he wanted to be humanitarian, he didn't want to be overrun by vermin. Can't blame him. Also, he told me, I was smaller than his own teenage daughter, so I shouldn't worry if he'd seen a piece or two of my skin. He was so kind and he probably saved my life.

But seeing the tidy room with its white down bedding, I think my body said to itself: this is it—safety. I think I'll throw the exhaustion party I've been thinking of for days, planning for days, fantasized for days, dreamed of for days.

I was delirious with fever for most of a week, and even though I was seriously malnourished, he later told me I wouldn't take any food at all at first. He tried oats and wheat. He got the doctor from the nearby town to come once and he said my prognosis was so-so, especially with what food was, or rather was not, available. The doctor wanted me to have meat broth, beef broth would be best. Would chicken or rabbit broth do? Gerhard asked. Apparently yes. Still, he also managed to get some bones from the butcher in town, which he boiled and improved with salt and herbs.

Gerhard told me later when he saw me stumble into his barn, he took it as some kind of sign and vowed to take care of me. Then he would take my getting well as a sign from God that things would get well on the farm again, too. We were to be a simultaneous project, me and his farm.

Because it was summer, it almost looked like his farm rallied faster than I did.

It was his teenage daughter's bedroom and bed that I slept in. Helga. But she lived with her mother in Hannover— they were seldom here, both disliking farm life, and he'd been living with them in the city for the last few years until he, too, was called up for service, but so late that he never saw action. And he'd come back to revive the farm because it was there, it was theirs, and it might be a security against all kinds of food shortage and other shortages that were likely to come about in the near future.

I wanted to do something to help, but I was a zero at farm work.

I did a few things, starting with sewing new curtains for the entire house. And I cooked most meals, though he was by far the better cook. I remember him making onions with liver he had somehow obtained at the butcher shop. And apples. He was a charmer, is a charmer. He gets everything he wants.

At first hanging out with Gerhard was easy and lovely because of his indomitable spirit. Yes, he'd get everything he really wanted, from everyone.

He never wanted me, though, not the way a man wants a woman. This was good and bad, both. Good because it spared us great discomfort; bad because it underlined my absolute insignificance in this life.

He says while I was in my fever and hallucinations, I would call the name Erich. He thought I was calling to him, and for a while he would try to correct me that his name was Gerhard, but I kept turning and twisting and calling for Erich.

"Your husband?" Gerhard asked when I was lucid again. I nodded. I couldn't speak. My throat was closed.

"He's no longer alive?" he asked, interpreting my difficulty speaking.

I shook my head.

"When did he die?"

"In 1916, a French . . . a prisoner of war," I said. I remember Gerhard's intake of breath.

"Not what you thought," I said.

"No. I thought more recently, this war. It's your second war then."

"Yours, too," I said.

"I was just a kid then." He nodded. "You have children?"

"Three," I said.

"They are well?" he asked.

"They were in February."

I told Gerhard once how I used to brush my hair, a hundred brush strokes each night, and he went and found a brush for me. It had a mother of pearl pattern on the handle. Such beautiful flakes of shimmer mystery.

I am afraid of the endless secrets we live. I wish I could meet Gerhard as a human being, without any hiding. I am afraid of this endless dishonesty that we force on each other—as though we were critters, strangers to each other, and we endlessly mess with each other's peace of mind.

I had a hard time writing again today. There's so much I still want to capture, but instead I went into Gerhard's forest again. Mulling over everything.

I felt ashamed, or perhaps guilty more than ashamed, that I didn't vigorously search for everyone. What was it? I feel distant. I feel guilty that I have brought them into this world which is a cruel world. Yes, it has given them laughter and light. And also so much cruelty. It just keeps going on and on and on. One cruelty after another. One torment after another. One hunger after another.

Sometimes I feel like a skeleton.

I have so much hatred for others in my life. Why are these hatreds so very prevalent? They seem to stick to me constantly, like burrs. Whereas the beautiful parts, people like Gerhard, are like a light mantle that is easily ignored, shrugged off, and then forgotten.

I am sixty-one years old. Why am I not in charge of my life?

Gerhard and Gabi are my shining, saving lights in this dark world.

I wonder what Gerhard's wife is like. She looks imposing on the handful of photos Gerhard showed me. I don't like her without even knowing her. I think she's not worthy of him. I've known people like that. They are chronically better than others. Her daughter no doubt is the best daughter in the world; her cherries no doubt are better than other people's cherries. Meanwhile there are people like me. I want recognition, too, but I have been meticulously trained to be humble, to let others be first. To let others be better.

Oh, how I hate them.

Oh, how I hate my own judgment.

I cannot focus. I want to keep hold of all these lovely ideas and insights I have, but instead I am full of fear and unease.

"My children are better than your children."

I think in a lot of ways I have done my children a great disservice by not bragging about them. I wish I had now. It is such a strange thing to be trained to be modest, and to pass that burden along.

Monika is the one who really makes me feel guilty. She's so clumsy in her great faith in the Lord. It's like she's lumbering along on a huge crutch she has selected and now that's how she walks through the world, awkwardly. And forbidding in her enlightened sternness.

I would never dare tell her about my thoughts. She'd judge them and I'd be too tired to defend them. Then she'd no doubt recommend some pious panacea. As a result, with her I will always be slightly dishonest. I can't stand lectures. From my own daughter or from anyone else.

Gabi doesn't lecture. Gabi only turns away and distances herself.

It's a wounded world when you cannot talk openly to your own children.

So often I don't want to be who I am. Judgmental, cold, and bristly. I thought it was required. I wish I could be as warm and alive as someone like Gerhard.

I was so sad when the village "discovered" we were living together. This promptly stopped everything that was excellent. The moral guard stepped in.

I would have rather kept on living with him on his farm. But the villagers determined that it just wouldn't do. I had to move in with the Leitners who graciously offered me a room and meals in return for household chores.

Gerhard taught me so much, about warmth, about being decent, and when I had to move on, I wasn't nearly done learning. He told me he saw no direct action in war. Still, he was there. It feels like we women are always kept in the background of hunger and ineffectual sobbing.

There is a sweetness, a gentleness that comes from suffering. What did Gerhard see that has made him so gentle? He only told me of one young soldier who was shot in the back for surrendering to the Americans. Like the three young men hanged in town. I guess nobody hanged or shot women.

"It could have been me," he said. "I was ready to surrender." Yes, it does make one feel lucky to be alive.

It is a horrible world where we feel compelled to punish survivors just for having the great luck to be able to keep on living in youth and in flower.

I wish I believed in God. If I did, I would pray that I may never be destroyed or have my humanity destroyed in the grip of envy or other ill will and vengefulness.

Gerhard was in the untrained reserve, called up late. *Volkssturm*, all men age sixteen to sixty had to go in October of 1944. Gerhard always was a pacifist at heart, but there came this time when he had no choice.

I don't want to be as dark as I am. I wasn't born to be this dark. I was born to live and love life. I wake up cringing against the awkwardness of having to take my place in the human world of interaction again. I ought to be joyous. I ought to be ecstatic.

It's easy. My daughters are here. Now all I have to do is finish packing. There's not much to pack. I can go with them, no problem. I do not want to. Seeing them again is amazing, indescribable. And yet I don't want to be with them. Gabi is beautiful. I didn't expect her to come. Something old-forgotten burned like a gentle flame in my chest.

It is so strange. My last little one, my last greeting from Erich, my last gift from the past. She's so beautiful, so young, so lovely.

I watch her. Monika is more of a talker. It is such a luxury for both of them to come, almost a waste.

Gabi's words: "Of course I'd come."

What a miracle to see her again. She has a beautiful light in her eyes. Gerhard invited us to the farm and all three of us went. I looked at everything through Gabi's eyes.

"You made these curtains? They're beautiful."

Now I don't know what will happen. Monika works in a hospital and they have promised her that I could have some work with them if I came. I wonder what it will be. Kitchen, or cleaning, or nurse's aide perhaps. So that's what will happen. Gabi is helping out in a grocery store. Her love affairs? None. I believe she is very attractive. She's too beautiful to be a spinster, but I don't know, she's not interested in men, though they're always interested in her. I hope I haven't caused that in her somehow.

I've watched her with Gerhard. She doesn't flirt. Nothing. Even Monika tries, makes an effort to make herself agreeable to Gerhard. Not Gabi. They'll both be spinsters. Maybe it's for the best.

Gerhard is the one who has taught me kindness.

At first the sight of Gabi gave me such a warm fire in my chest.

Why do I have no passion? I am so lost in this world. I have forgotten what I want and who I am, and so I am no longer a viable human being.

Strange. Sad. Sickening.

Why did I have to be so turned to stone, like in a fairy tale of old? It didn't profit anyone.

That is what witches do in fairy tales—they turn you to stone and you have to, if at all possible, avoid it. I have tried. I have not been successful. I should not have allowed this turning to stone. Once upon a time I had such longing for life and now I have none.

I wouldn't dream of telling my daughters this. It is not necessary that they know the truth, that I am old, and that the only glimmer of fire left in me is anger and indignation and perhaps a small light of pride, though I am suspicious of the concept of pride. The thousands and thousands of death notices: "In proud sorrow." How can you be proud of the death of your fathers, brothers, husbands, sons?

When Erich left, I tried to keep the children indifferent—I'd seen it with others, hugging their fathers' knees and not wanting to let go. What a farce. I didn't want him to go, no. I believe all war is an atrocity, no matter what. People who wear different clothes to be able to tell each other apart killing the ones with the other clothes. How is that sensible? It is stupid. It is evil.

And yet in the twenties I had to take on military assignments, making armbands, putting emblems on brown shirts and hats. I had to feed my children by promoting this new national pride that then not ten years later led us back into a misery that was already all too familiar. Now we have to do it all over again. Except this time, today . . . .

I was interrupted. Gabi left. She had only taken off the weekend and two days surrounding it.

She is so beautiful. I could stare at her for hours. No, she looks nothing like me. She looks much stronger.

Gerhard's farm is in good shape now. Even a flock of white geese. Thank you, life. I wish I knew better what to do.

I feel bereft.

It has not been easy for me. It has also not been more difficult than it has been for others. The sun rises every morning. I am grateful for the memories. I am grateful for my daughters and that they looked for me and came for me. I am grateful Tillmann and his wife and two of his children are alive.

Every day the same ache, though, the same agony.

My bags are packed. There is only one thing left to do: go and burn these pages. I thought I would want to keep them. I was mistaken. They have turned too dark, so I will go and burn my darkness, turn it over to God and the world. God already knows. How I have done my best. How I once wanted to praise and bring joy and love into the world. How I have been challenged by the bitterness of the world. How I have been conquered by the world. How it became a horror around me.

I wish I had the hopeful energy of youth. I do not have it. Things have become dark. Maybe they always were that. I smile at people. I do try to hide the darkness. It is the best I can do. Life is good to me. I am moving. My fingers grasp, my lungs are breathing. It is a miracle to be alive. I am amazed that with this miraculous being we do not constantly all sing. The darkness. I keep trying to hide the darkness that has been imposed on me, the bitterness. The responsibility or else the duty to watch all this. We build worlds and then we smash them. It seems so foolish.

I try to smile and be kind. For Gerhard's sake. For Erich's sake. I wonder if Erich's spirit is out there watching over us. So many of us dreamers dream of this.

The darkness is so huge.

In the past I have gone on new adventures, I have survived losses, I have gone on and on. Now I am tired. Monika says I'll sleep with her in her room at first. I can work a little to earn my keep, and eventually I'll get my own room. I should be excited. I am exhausted instead.

I am grateful to Gerhard for keeping me alive.

I am afraid of the future.

I am old and lost in this life that should have been beautiful.

I have made so many mistakes, and perhaps the greatest of all is that I have thought too much about all these things, that I have hoped too much, that I have seen the potential for enormous beauty and then have witnessed the incurable starkness of our misguided world. I am so filled with horror.

I want to be gone now. It is best to throw out my writing. I thought I could preserve my freedom with it somehow. But I cannot.

God, what have you done to us? We have invented you for solace and for inspiration, and then it turns out we just use you to justify each other's cruelties.

If I had the right mind, it would be hot inside my breast from endless gratitude. As it is, I am just cringing with a sense of wanting to be done.

There was a progression life should have had. A beauty. It didn't happen. Instead of flowering, we dry up and kill each other out of resentment. Maybe if I had been a man with even more angry spirit, I would also have started wars instead of whimpering like this and nursing dark thoughts of disappointment until they poison me and numb me from the inside. Blessings to you, Erich, for having been my companion in early life. Blessings to you, Gerhard, for saving my life in the end. Blessings to you, my children, for making me strong enough to go on, over and over and over, without just giving up in the face of so much darkness. It is time to go on and be brave some more. To read a few poems, to laugh a few laughters.

Today we leave.

I will now walk up to the hill behind Gerhard's barn and bury these pages. I can't burn them now after all, not in the middle of summer. It would draw too much attention. I thought of dropping them into the well, but that would probably cause problems. With all my bitterness, it might just outright poison the well.

I love you, world, despite everything. Goodbye.

I did ask the Leitners about Gerhard's wife. Snooty is how Mrs. Leitner finally described her. Too bad.

Anger isn't allowed to a woman. But it is there. Anger at the ease with which nations declare and conduct war. Kill our men.

I do not like this anger that is boiling in me all the time, and anger always survives.

My parents were in their fifties when Erich died. So I went to live with them with the children.

It is like a bunch of boys—and they are allowed to act out their anger by putting on some uniform or another and stand opposite each other with shotguns and just have at it. No longer even sword or dagger.

We make it wholesale death.

I wasn't raised to anger.

I was raised to sorrow. Sorrow was permitted. Grief was permitted, but in a lot of ways, grief hasn't happened. Anger was stronger. Anger stopped me short of grief and sadness. I could never get beyond anger. I am grateful to my anger. It kept me strong and functional where grief might have devastated me. Then what would have happened to my children? I felt I was responsible for them. And what have I accomplished? One is a church mouse, the other a young intellectual spewing rebel energy into the world, and finally the third, the boy, a soldier—now out of work, but with enough vitality to go on and make a living. Somehow.

Anger trumps everything.

It is the only thing occasionally bursting out of the cold wall I have built around myself.

What is behind my wall?

Oh, only my life's search, my deep love for a world that is so beautiful and so marred by its human inhabitants.

Another secret: my deep love for Erich who, like me, like so many others, wasn't given much of a choice in anything. I praise the world for letting us be together, if only for a little while. As colleagues, as competitors for my father's favor and for my father's projects. And sometimes, for a moment, I am able to forget the present and I am able to love him again.

Erich was originally a paid apprentice in my father's shop. At first I didn't want to have anything to do with him. I didn't want to be part of a cliché. The apprentice and the master's daughter. But I liked him. So did my father.

It took us long enough to get married. I guess my inner Gabi, too, was quite reluctant.

In any event, I won't lack for grandchildren, as Tillmann has already two sons. The little girl, Monika told me, died on the trip. Pneumonia. "The name will go on, though," she said. What do I care? It's not my name or my father's name.

He was fourteen and I was eleven when he first came to be my father's apprentice. I'd give him plums and cherries when they were in season. After the first reluctance, I adored him, never having had a sibling. All the other apprentices that came and went over the years, they were ugly or dumb, or both. With Erich there was a light, always. At Christmas time I gave him hazelnut cookies. Once he gave me an orange. I was so in love with him. Then he went away to work in other places, to seek his fortune. He went as far as Berlin and always promised to take me there one day. He never did, and I've never been. Then he was conscripted, late, he was in his thirties already; everybody was always assuming the war would be over quickly, that stupid first war.

I remember when he returned from his years in Berlin. He felt like such a stranger, and so handsome. I asked him once, what were the girls like in Berlin? His words were a quick caress. "I don't remember," he said. "I was always thinking of you." I knew this was probably not true, but saying it made me feel treasured.

I was meant to love and to be sentimental. I don't know what I would have become, had I been allowed to be who I might have been.

I was meant to be joyous in this world, grow violets, travel the world with my love.

I was meant to be young, forever young and beautiful.

I wish we could have shared those years he was gone but still in this life.

I have to go. Goodbye.

STRANGE JUSTICE

I imagine Pétain's hands shake when he eats. But I forget, we're not to use his name anymore. We're to call him the condemned man in the citadel. I am the woman who makes his soup. I like to use tomatoes and other things that stain. Of course only his wife sees him anyway when she comes for her daily visit, or his nurse, or the physicians. In the end, it doesn't matter much.

At age eighty-nine they sentenced him to death. He had collaborated with the Germans. But his sentence was changed at once. Imprisonment instead. Now, at ninety-two, he is alive, and I slice meat for his soup and boil bones. If I leave in pieces of gristle instead of feeding them to the cat, or if pieces are left half-raw, he doesn't even notice. At least I haven't heard.

I hope he is bored in his two rooms of confinement, with a view of the changeless sea and sand and stone, after being a military man in command for fifty, sixty, seventy years. And I, who am free to come and go, I also go nowhere, and I have only one room to share with the cat. As a girl I knew a story of lovers waiting for each other by the sea. This sea is nothing like that.

De Gaulle changed the death sentence. I wonder why. Maybe because the old man would die soon anyway. Or to let the good God take him when the good God willed. Or perhaps the old man got credit for serving his country so well one war earlier, this hero of Verdun in World War I. Sometimes when I lie awake at night, I wonder, to the ceaseless droning of the sea, how they would have executed him. Would they have shot him? Used gas? Later they symbolically executed a tree in his stead, which makes me angry when I think about it. It feels like mockery. I can't even imagine how one executes a tree. Would that be different from felling it just for furniture or wood for the stove? Sometimes I think we are all crazy.

Of one thing I am sure: dying doesn't hurt much, or at least not for long. It is living that hurts. Living with wounds, with injustice, with loss. It's raw, always raw, like the meat I slice for his soup. When I brush my hair in the morning, I brush the hair of a mask, a mannequin, something that moves and functions without will. I look in the mirror and I can't understand what I see. I'm not who I expected to be. I merely lug around the flesh and bones of someone I should have been.

I've never met the old man face to face.

Perhaps he doesn't care. Good for him, no? Some say he never cared for anything or anyone, that he was utterly unmoved by any suffering he saw. Ice-cold, they say. Some say it's a crime all the same to keep a man his age in prison. As for me, I never say a word to anyone.

I wonder if he has bedsores, what he remembers from his life, and if he has regrets.

Moths knock on my window at night. Those that find their way inside fold their wings into the shape of a heart before they die. What do moths die from? Maybe old age or lack of fresh air. I hope they knock on his windows, too, to keep him awake on endless nights.

So I keep making his soup, day after day. It's always women making the soup, except in the middle of the war out at the front, or in fancy hotels, when there's a reputation to be got. Then men might cook.

Why didn't I refuse to cook for him? Because I, too, have to eat. I have to live. I have no children. My love was killed too early. I don't know what else to do. I would have begged for Lucien's life on my knees, but I didn't get a chance. I didn't even know until it was already over.

So I make soup. That's who I am. I cut meat. The tendons, too. I make sure they go in the old man's broth. As though it mattered. Gristle and tendons, my puny offerings of hatred.

I once was in love. Now I merely have my life and the cat. The soup. The hatred. The endless consciousness.

Perhaps I like to be near the old man because he reminds me of Lucien. But that's nonsense. I need no reminders. Each day of my life I have thought of Lucien. As for the rest, I'm just there. Alive. Conscious. That's all.

My name is Natalie. Only one person has ever called me Tati, my precious Lucien with his black lock of hair falling on his forehead. He was a charmer, popular with all the girls. Still, he never made me feel insecure. Of course he never got much of a chance to prove himself faithful.

He didn't even go to military school or anything like that. One day he was just called up. And so he had to go.

Lucien Leblanc. Lucien and Natalie Leblanc. We weren't officially promised yet. All the same, we knew we would marry one day. He was twenty when he died. So was I. I'm fifty-three now.

I'm heavy with dull hatred. Hatred isn't even bitter. It's tasteless. It fills me, but it doesn't satisfy. My hatred is bland, and with it I cook an old man's soup. All the same, the hatred eats me, not him.

Why don't I poison him? I could easily do it so no one would know. But I want him to keep suffering from life, which is itself a sort of poison. Some say it's inhuman the way he is treated. He's probably the oldest prisoner on earth. But he lives. Lucien does not.

Even wishing suffering on him does me no good. My loathing is like a tired bag of bones. I am unmoved, cold, and mechanical.

And why don't I poison myself? I've thought of that, too. But I don't want to die, despite being useless to myself. Sometimes I feel uneasy when I watch myself just yearning for the morsels of bread, and the milk and the water, or even just the sight of green grass, or sparrows pecking between stones, or the feel of the cat at my feet.

I've never told a soul that I'm cooking for *the* one. They'd accuse me of being a patsy. Could be. I do want to live, for the taste of the bread, for the hopping of the sparrows on the courtyard stones. That makes me the same as every woman on earth who cooks soup for others who live.

The crazy part is, he, Pétain, they claim, didn't fight against his death sentence. Only his advocates did. How would he have died? Would he have been afraid? Would there have been an audience? It would have happened in a clean and humane way, somehow, and he couldn't have cared less.

Lucien cared, and he was put to death for it. It won't do, in this world, to want to—to be sane enough to want to—live.

I remember Lucien coming through the trees to me to our hidden meeting place in the forest. The trees seemed taller than any trees I know of. Perhaps because he, my Lucien, seemed so small in front of them. He was laughing against the backdrop of all that green. He was almost always laughing.

"There you are."

He picked me up and swung me in a circle. My feet whipped against shrubs, and I squealed with joy, and then we sat next to each other and kissed.

We didn't do anything else. We were waiting until we were married.

Lucien was always so happy, always in a good mood, even about their plans.

"War doesn't make sense for the likes of us," he said. He and twenty-four others had a plan to get them back to their fields, to their lives. He said he couldn't tell me what it was. "But it will work. You'll see."

"You have to tell me," I said. "Now you've made me worry."

"I can't tell you. It's a sort of a secret between the others and myself."

"What on earth is 'a sort of a secret'?" I asked. "It's either a secret or not. Did you swear not to tell?"

"No."

"That means you can tell me. Besides, you can trust me. I won't repeat it."

He blushed as he told me. They were going to shoot their own hands, all twenty-five of them. They'd then have to be dismissed as unfit for military service.

"But it will hurt," I said.

Not as much as other things would hurt, he said, and then he blushed even deeper. "Also, I don't want to kill anybody."

Over the years, I'm never sure I remember the conversation correctly. I've tried to. Maybe I added some words or left some out.

"Can't they send you somewhere else?" I asked him. "Where you could still serve, without shooting yourself?"

"No, Tati," he said. "I can't even read and write properly. Certainly not enough to be of any use to anyone in an office."

I shook my head. "But you're good with animals," I said.

I suddenly wanted to make love with him. I offered myself.

"No," he said, clutching my hand. "We'll wait. It's important to wait and do it right." To him it was a sacred thing.

"It would still be sacred," I insisted. "I swear."

He picked three sprigs of heather and handed them to me. "You don't know how hard it is not to," he said.

I didn't understand, except that he somehow wanted me to be strong. Anyway, he kissed me gently, and a few times not so gently, and we rubbed against each other a bit, and it felt wonderful, and I thought it couldn't get much better anyway, so this seemed like a sensible compromise at getting what I wanted.

The best part of their plan was that there were so many of them. You couldn't punish that many infantrymen all at once, especially when they were wounded. The loss would be too great. Or so they thought. The worst, Lucien feared, was that they might be called cowards afterwards. If they did, he wanted to know, would I be able to live with that?

"I know you're not a coward, Lucien," I said. Some of the others might well have been cowards, but not Lucien. I didn't want to think of any others at all.

I didn't see Lucien again. One moment he stood at one of the trees with a twinkle in his eyes, his head slightly cocked to the left. "*À bientôt*," he said. See you soon. Then the branches closed between us.

Things happened quickly after that.

His parents were notified. They didn't say a word to anyone. It took a while for one of my brothers to ferret it out. As planned, the twenty-five men had shot themselves into their own hand or arm to avoid being sent to the front. So Pétain had all twenty-five of them bound and driven to the enemy trenches. He might as well have shot them himself. Not one of them survived. Served them right was the consensus of shaky whispers. But behind that judgment, I'm sure, many a survivor crossed himself, and blessed his fate for being too old, too weak, too useless to have to make that kind of choice himself.

Sometimes I imagine the old man—he was only fifty-nine then—livid with rage at the riffraff, these boys under his command who dared to try to live in spite of what he asked of them. He treated them like bugs you step on, young men who would rather cheat than die. He later executed others, too. But him they allow to live. If he had been in charge of his own punishment, he would have made short shrift.

For a while I was obsessed with wanting to know who had driven Lucien and the others to the trenches. As though it mattered. In my mind I would plead with them in retrospect. Don't drive them there. Don't drive them to their certain death. They aren't even the enemy. They are your own people.

In the village, there was outrage. People should have known better, I thought. His own parents were tight-lipped with embarrassment. They should have been loyal to Lucien. They turned their backs on me, too, when I tried to go to them for comfort.

So many aching dreams, so many hindsight fantasies. I miss Lucien. He has been gone for over thirty years.

Eventually I couldn't bear the village anymore. I left. Things were hard then anyway. Food was scarce. As young men went missing left and right, nobody missed one young woman more or less.

Lucien was right about one thing. What little I could read and write was of no great use to me, and I knew far more than Lucien ever did. I earned my keep as a cleaning woman for many years, and sometimes as a cook. Once, in Nantes, I had a job as a flower shop girl for a very short time. But they told me if I didn't make an effort to flirt with the young men a bit, they'd have to let me go. So they let me go. It made no sense. Weren't these guys there to buy flowers for their sweethearts? Then why did I need to flirt with them, too? But apparently that's how it was done.

And here I am. Safely and bitterly stranded, alive on this god-forsaken island, cooking for a prisoner.

"Je t'aime." That was always my line with Lucien. I love you.

"Moi aussi," he said once more from the edge of the forest. That was always his line. Me too.

And so, even when it doesn't feel right, I cook for the survivor in exchange for my own morsels of life. Nothing has ever felt right since Lucien died.

Sometimes I think of the cost of food, the cost of living. How strange that often, when people grow old, we throw them away, like stuff that's been used up. But not this one. Every time I turn around, there's somebody else pleading for mercy, for better treatment for the old man, as he drags his awkward body through a partisan world with lawyers and spokesmen. Perhaps God has condemned him to live the years he has stolen from others.

I look at my hands. The cat presses against my legs for her share. Smells good, doesn't it? There's a moth on the floor, kitty. There, just in front of your nose. Not good enough, eh? Well, here's a piece of meat then. Go away now. Go on.

WHORE

I am sorry you feel that way, my son.

Life wounds.

My parents said I had to go and so I went. I was still obedient then. I suppose I still am.

On the way to the camp I missed my two younger sisters so much. Once I was there and given my duties, I forgot even my sisters. That was no place for sweet memory. There was only time for pain, anger, hatred, shame, despair. There was only time for disbelief that I had to be there and had to do what I had to do. I swore then that I had no family any longer, and I have kept that vow. Not that it does any good.

I have no family except your father who is sorry that he married a whore.

I have no family except you, my son, who are sorry that your mother was a whore.

I have no family except my decaying self that is sorry I have to live like this.

I once was a young girl. I once had such dreams.

You once were a young boy. You once had such dreams. Maybe you dreamt of being a foundling. Maybe your true mother was a secret princess who had to abandon you for your own good. Then you came home from school into a kitchen smelling of cabbage and bacon and grits, and you knew you had neither choice nor hope. We were it. Your father who drank and your mother who cringed or yelled obscenities, and the sad part is, the more I yelled, the less he beat me to try and pass along his pain. When I tried to be pleasant, it didn't go well for us.

But you know what? Maybe I was a princess once. In that long forsworn family that sent me on my way.

I gave your father one brilliant moment of glory—when he decided he would save me out of that hellhole where men lined up outside of the tent to come spill their seed, all of them eager to do it, and all of them disgusted that they had to do it like that. I could swear when he asked me, his brown eyes shone with nobility and his spirit flew around him like a dove.

It didn't last, this spirit, this shining.

I know I was luckier than most. I do not know why he chose me. I didn't ask. He never said. I was no prettier than any of the others. I was no more skillful than any of the others. I guess it was the lottery of life.

I feel like a decaying rose that never bloomed.

I want to say to you, let us bow our heads and pray. But such words seem too delicate for this gritty life.

Before you went to school where you were taunted and also praised, we had one sunny day by the river. I will not forget. I fed you plum cakes. You likely don't remember, no. Sunlight played with the water, brilliant shivers of light.

I had moments of light as a child, too. All children, I believe, own buckets full of laughter. But I have vowed to forget that family.

Maybe I, too, should learn to forgive. I do not know how.

After we learn to love again, it will be easier.

COLORS

Sylvie came with the dawn that divides the light from dark without yet distinguishing them. Marie smiled with relief when she held her new baby in her arms and all the physical exhaustion swam away in a flood of tingling respite. Her nerves were so still that the stillness itself sang to her senses, while all around her the blurred patches of pain receded to the pleasure of white peacefulness. The walls were white, the sheets, the pillows, the sprigs of flowers her husband had brought. She wished she could hold on to the light of that moment.

When Erika died, the world had turned gray, dull with duty, a way of carrying it around on living shoulders, with a living heart mechanically beating out its logic. Just before the death things had been mercilessly colorful, a mad farewell to frenzy. Deciding to get on the train to the West before the Russians came. The last train ever it turned out. Frantically sorting what to leave behind. So little could be taken. The rich brown oak of the table and beds, left behind. The second best silver, left behind. The green velvet curtains, left behind.

In the icy air of early March, Erika caught a cold, then shrank away into herself, too small to make the effort to hang on. She coughed up sounds of retching blood before she ever learned the language of the living. For three days and nights her body faded, until at last it stiffened in Marie's thin arms.

Then the train stopped. Occupation soldiers brought chocolate and demanded the dead, mostly children. Hygienic reasons. And the women delivered. Seventeen dead, most of them children, and most of those babies, on one single train. The mothers were allowed to come to the steps of the train, Marie among them, but no further, and no one else. There was no time for ceremony, and they could not stay. The last vivid flash of color in Marie's senses was the sight of her wedding veil, wrapped around Erika's lifeless body, to distinguish her from the rest with large cotton flowers in lace. She forced her fingers to let go of the small body, to let it be taken to a shared grave. Then Marie had to go inside the train again, herded toward the living, to do the stuff that living people did, nothing of great significance. One day, she swore, she would return.

Sylvie grew up with ruins for playgrounds. From time to time you heard news of bomb shells, deeply wedged into the ground, exploding. After a time, Marie, like other mothers, learned to ignore anxiety. All you could do was tell the children to be careful, and, if they noticed anything like craters, to report it to an adult immediately. You explained what craters were. There were flowers in the ruins, even fancy ones from former gardens mixed in with invincible dandelions and goldenrod.

In truth, the color of hatred was glaring, like a terrible fire with no one watching, no one to know. Marie walked in the woods and scanned the ground for beetles, vermin she could step on. Once she squashed a small toad with the heel of her shoe, convulsively shaking with the sensation of the throbbing life stamped flat into the ground, liquid color licking up into her brain. And you, God, see this: I also can kill. I also can end life. And still the hatred licked, alive like malicious laughter inside, scathing, burning, yet cleansing nothing, not even the wound.

So it was better that the world should turn gray with duty, with the technicalities of living. Tying her shoelace, trading her ration of butter for a sack of flower at the mill. At home, standing before her younger sister, fierce like a lioness, with the low tone of growling in her voice, while the words she spoke were polite and precise, and the solid man wiped the leer off his face, tipped his hat, turned, and walked away. That sort of courage had no color, just a dutiful act, an involuntary shield. Better the world should be gray.

One day, on the tram, Sylvie sang the national anthem she had learned in school that day. "Be quiet," Marie said harshly. "Someone might hear." A few weeks and many silences later she corrected Sylvie's misunderstanding. Not all songs were forbidden in public. Just this one. And that even though the unspeakable words of pride, *"Deutschland, Deutschland über alles,"* had safely been relegated to the last of three verses, leaving an inoffensive trinity of unity and justice and freedom up front.

The hardest for Marie was her husband. It should have felt miraculous to hold him in her arms after the long and lonely fears. Instead she felt the ache of a series of gnawing, voiceless twistings of the mind. You, husband, I accuse you of your daughter's death. She's gone. You never even saw her once. True, you were no longer drinking champagne in Paris and slurping oysters when she was born. But you were still conducting your war. You still marched in formation, your snappy ballet of murder, when she died. These thoughts were throbbing in her mind and had to be endured. Better that they should be gray and dull inside a shelter of duty.

Worse yet was when Sylvie got ill, again and again, then recovered, time after time. Aside from her feelings of mercy and triumph, Marie resented her new daughter's luxury. Cradled in comfort, she could survive with camphor inhalations and chamomile infusions. What would it take to smash her fragile body to make her join her sister who had never even had a chance? Or she could simply leave her unattended, too small and weak to fend for herself with her complicated diseases. Electrified by her thoughts, Marie would turn to her work again, changing sheets that were splattered with vomit and soaked with perspiration, feeding the girl spoon after spoonful of chamomile tea. Such thoughts had to be drained of their color to make room for the routine.

Once every year, on a Sunday in March, they took a train to the village where Erika had been placed in her mass grave with its modest commemorative marker. They didn't take young Sylvie. That was no place for children who lived. The dead ones lay together under one small mound near the wall of the graveyard, the stones of the wall crumbling in that corner, and one large wooden nameless cross, already weathered, over the grave.

Then there was the year when Sylvie did have to come. There was no place to leave her. It was a mistake from the first. The child seemed to think this was a pleasure excursion. Marie wiped a tear from her face, then another. She hadn't cried much when it had happened. There hadn't been time. Tears are not duty, they are luxury. Sylvie didn't even kneel or stand still, but jumped up to touch a butterfly. She asked why this wasn't like graves in the city, with interesting tombstones with moss in the crevices, musty, and bearing carved names. Her father told her how Erika was now with the angels and angels didn't need names. It didn't look like Sylvie was content with the explanation, this unfairness of such an insignificant place for her sister when total strangers had much better ones.

Marie watched her disappointed daughter pout and try to come to grips as they walked away from the graveyard. The sun was already high up in the sky and still rising.

"I don't think we need to come back again," Marie said to her husband.

He took a deep breath and agreed. For the first time she noticed that some of his hair had turned white. And how red the ribbons were in Sylvie's brown hair. How the green pushed itself into buds on the trees. The sun kept rising to illuminate it all from changing angles in the sky.

THE GOOD GUYS

A photo of her hometown, 1945. The castle in the background, standing. The church transparent with boldly missing chunks of stone, but the basic structure is intact. The rest is rubble, ragged stones that no longer look manmade. One five story façade stands tall, facing the market with nothing behind it, no depth, no life, no commerce. All back to nature almost, with grass already growing wild between the tumbled bricks.

However, the market square is filled with striped umbrellas—red and white mostly she remembers, though the photo is black and white. Commerce has resumed with eggs and vegetables and, yes, a few flowers for those whose life continues. Women with shopping bags, men striding with produce or purpose, children quite possibly laughing. One perky umbrella has polka dots.

She used to play in the ruins nearby. Splendid places for hide and seek, always provided there were no longer any not yet exploded bombs.

The rubble patiently sits in the grass awaiting the future. Peace at a cost. The work of the good guys.

Not her favorite photo, perhaps, but one that haunts her with impatience for a time when women and men will have the courage to persuade each other that priceless peace is far better than what the good guys do.

ISIS

At some point you held cows sacred, didn't you? And in places they still do—to an extent, but it isn't as it used to be. Mostly "cow" is used as insult now. In Germany, for example, they call a dull-witted woman—or whoever they think is one—a dumb cow. If she's sprightly, but still offensive, they might call her a stupid she-goat instead. The only term of stupidity that includes both genders would be a camel.

Meanwhile, an acclaimed Scottish ballroom dancer once called his slender partner—who was stunning, though not pretty—a fat cow just to hurt her. It probably worked, though there wasn't an ounce of fat on her bones. Like most contemporary women she was most likely afraid of the specter of that horrifying ounce and spent a good deal of her precious life fighting against its threat, feeling each day of deprivation and struggle and physical weakness a triumph of calories counted, rather than counting her accomplishments or ecstasies.

But I digress. You may or may not know the story of how I came to wear a cow's head. In short, my brother Seth—greedy, moody, and jealous, as some gods simply are—killed our mutual brother, Osiris, who was also my beloved husband. Sibling rivalry is the root of most evil, though I should perhaps say fraternal rivalry. Sisters aren't well documented for killing one another or their brothers. In any case, Seth ended up killing Osiris not just once, but twice, because I managed to revive Osiris the first time. But Seth found him again when I wasn't watching and hacked him into fourteen pieces. I searched for them with our other sister, Nephthys, and I found them all except for his penis. So I put my husband together again and replaced the missing piece with a golden one. (The original, in case you want to know, turned out to have been swallowed by a fish—who then in turn mysteriously swallowed itself. An Egyptian puzzle if you ever saw one!) I can imagine some smart-aleck woman say to her lover, "If I'd been Isis, I would have kept looking."

Anyway, we gods do what we can. And I did become pregnant by Osiris, even after he was slain. I carried our cherished son Horus. For a while there, Seth kept me imprisoned and I sat in a little prison cell weaving for him and teaching the women he tried to rule. He ruled with considerable difficulty because of his moods and his previously mentioned propensity for jealousy. But when Horus was about to be born I escaped and hid and raised my son.

Then Osiris managed to come from the other world to teach our son, and eventually Horus was strong enough to challenge his uncle Seth for the throne, which was of course what the killing of Osiris earlier on had been all about.

Horus and Seth fought for eighty years. Yes, you heard that right, eighty years. Sometimes one would have the upper hand, then the other. Once I interfered out of pity for Horus and helped him out, which he appreciated very much. And then later I interfered and helped out Seth out of pity as well, which saved Seth's life that time. This upset Horus so much that he turned against me and cut off my head. Not long afterwards, Horus felt sorry about this impulsive rage against me and put a cow's head on my neck. That's how I came by my cow's head.

But, as I said, that was then and this is now. Cows are out of fashion now, except for meat and milk, which most people take for granted and don't treat as anything special anymore—except in places where meat and milk are not so readily available, and in those areas they might still trade cows for women.

Ladies, I don't understand your world.

If I stood on the edge of a battlefield today, I would do exactly what I did before, and I would say to anyone who would question me, "He's my brother. He's my son."

You, my deluded and diluted sisters, stand by the battlefields as of old, with the same urgent horror in your bones. Only you don't interfere. Perhaps I could teach you. I was always good at teaching other women. Death has its place, but I am here to teach the living.

It's cold here at the edge of evil, blood and guts all around, the wind of ignorance howling. Perhaps I could howl louder yet.

He's your brother. He's your son.

Annette and Florian

In 1942 the Boches are everywhere, not just in Paris. The greatest fear is falling into their hands and coming to their special attention. Annette, make sure you practice your German phrases, and color your hair, every two weeks. Every two weeks, do you hear me?

Maman, my hair is practically falling out, it's brittle, and I hate the smell. Well, it's important, Annette. Mine's white already, but yours isn't, so it's important that you make it blond. If it's so important that we have a Jewish ancestor somewhere on Papa's side, then why don't we leave like others have done? Because, my darling, Papa is ill, and I am old, and we don't have a chance to start a new life elsewhere. Maman, I'm old enough, I'll take care of you both. We should go. Annette, it would kill Papa, and it might kill me, too. We're too old to start over.

So Annette colors her hair. The Boches now swarm all over Strasbourg and everybody lives under a cloud of fear. One day they come to Annette's house to interrogate her parents, but not Annette herself. Not yet, she assumes. She sits in the garden, crying with fear and with shame. And with frustration. And lack of hope.

"*Vous voyez comme une déesse,*" a man says behind her, and she is so taken by surprise that she laughs out loud despite her despair and in the face of all common sense. She quickly sobers up and tells him that she speaks German.

Immediately he asks, in German, why she laughed like that and she feels fear go through her like a blast turning all her muscles to mush. She can barely sit upright. She reaches for the closest tree to steady herself. He tells her to look at him and to tell him. So she looks at him and his eyes are kind.

"You said I see like a goddess," she explains. "You probably meant to say I look like one."

"Then you must teach me to keep my French in better order," he says.

"If you want me to."

"I do," he says. "I am Adjutant Fuchs. And you're the daughter of the house?"

She nods. She knows he is constantly keeping his eyes on her with a proprietary kind of gaze, and she in turn tries to look his way as little as possible. She hates her own submissiveness and knows it can't be helped. "I am called Annette Stein."

"Then you're really partly German," he says.

She doesn't say anything in response, but when he touches her arm, she trembles so much that she feels her skin is going to simply fly off her flesh.

For several weeks she teaches him French for an hour each day. He brings her presents of food at times and tobacco for her father, who doesn't smoke but hoards it to trade for other things. Her family is left alone, conspicuously so, because neighbors start to behave strangely, becoming more distant, which hurts her mother deeply. Annette can tell. Her father is too ill to be out and about much, so he hardly notices. Annette keeps dyeing her hair to a color Adjutant Fuchs declares more than once he thinks is beautiful. Little does he know.

It is summer, and as often as the weather and the long hours of daylight permit, they have their daily lesson outside. He is always polite. He starts calling her Annette. That seems only normal. He also tells her his first name, Florian. But coax as he will, she cannot possibly call him by his first name, much less can she use the informal form of address with him, "*tu*" or "*Du*," except in impersonal examples of language, of which he then proceeds to make quite a game. But in real life communications she addresses him formally, and, to her surprise, so does he with her, despite also continuing to call her by her first name. She starts trusting his good will, though his presence feels awkward to her, clumsy and heavy. Perhaps it is her fear of him as a Boche that makes her feel that way. One time he tries to kiss her, and she looks so terrified that he abandons the attempt, says a regretful two-syllable word, "*Naja*," and never repeats the attempt.

After four months he is called away from Strasbourg and stationed elsewhere. He leaves her and her family a large stash of tins of food. Then one night their house goes up in flames. Her father's weak heart doesn't make it through that night. There is a cursory investigation, but the fire isn't of any great importance at the time to anyone besides her and her mother, what with so many other war-time calamities occurring left and right. Her mother dies shortly afterwards, both of her parents long before the war finally ends, which end they would have enjoyed witnessing.

Annette gets by, living in a room she rents from a friendly unmarried school teacher. There is no money to have the house rebuilt. In fact, for the time being nobody has any money, not even to buy the land from her and develop it for themselves.

Life doesn't turn out to be what it had promised to be, or what she has, promise or no promise, believed it would be. She works as a seamstress in a small clothing factory, doing some of the finer needlework that can't be sent down the mechanical production line, not with the state of the art of then current machinery. Sometimes in the evenings she goes to visit the ruins of her old home and just sits there, looking into the past and trying to see the future. In the summer when the weather is nice she goes almost daily. She sits on the long stone wall that is left standing, cleaned now from ashes by years of rain and sanitized by the scorching of the sun.

One day in 1948, a shadow steps out from among fruit trees now left to grow wild for birds and squirrels and adventurous children who don't mind playing among the ruins.

"I couldn't forget you," he says. He is no longer Adjutant Fuchs, but plain Florian Fuchs. One of his arms is missing. He says it doesn't matter. He also says it doesn't matter about her hair, which is no longer blond, but dark brown, and, he insists, very attractive. He is now studying for the ministry and she is glad he is alive.

His presence still feels heavy to her. The whole situation feels heavy, with him stepping out of the trees after so much loss, after so much animosity and fear. She isn't sure what her feelings are exactly, but she is grateful for his willingness to be her friend, and she is touched by his tales of carrying her around in his heart even while they were officially each other's enemies.

They are married as soon as his theological studies are completed, and they decide to emigrate to the United States rather than staying in either one of their formerly warring countries. They are young enough for that kind of courage. They are young enough for the three children they create together. They are young enough to start a new existence, she in a country she already wanted to go to once anyway, and he in the ministry where he finds standing up for God a much gentler discipline than standing up for Hitler.

When they get to New York Harbor, having dutifully admired the Statue of Liberty with both anticipation and apprehension, they stand in the immigration office, separated by a wooden window frame from the immigration officer.

"You're Mr. and Mrs. Fuchs?" the officer asks.

"Yes."

"What does it mean?"

"Pardon?"

"Your name," the officer clarifies. His complexion is peculiarly ruddy. "Does it mean anything in English?"

"Yes. It means fox."

"Permit me to issue your green cards with the English name. Mr. and Mrs. Fox. Trust me. It is better."

They are confused, but feel obliged to trust him and certainly do not want to cause any trouble of delay or other inconvenience to themselves. If the immigration officer says they must be called Fox, then they will be called Fox. Later Florian changes his name, informally and for practical purposes, to Fred. Annette's name doesn't appear to be in need of any adjustments.

They spend a good twenty years together in the New Country, and he is much respected in the community despite his never quite eradicated German accent, which at first offends some people in his congregation because they have lost brothers, fathers, and sons on account of Hitler's ambitions. Annette is respected, too, but that is not surprising. The French hadn't offended anyone very deeply of late.

The last words he says to her before he dies are these: "*Vous voyez comme une déesse.*" Then she laughs and she cries and she believes that she has loved him all along, that dashing formerly blond man who has once made her tremble with such fear.

THE DEMONSTRATION

It's a pretty day today, but it's hot. I don't much like going to demonstrations with my Mom anymore. I used to like it a little better when I was smaller because it made me feel important. But now I'm usually bored and sometimes I'm embarrassed. I count squirrels and pigeons just so that I have something to do. There are three pigeons pecking on one large piece of French bread right now, trying to pull it apart, but they haven't managed yet. It looks kind of funny. And there are two squirrels chasing each other up a tree over on the other side of Broadway.

At first I was pretty bored today, too. And I know it's a sin to be bored at an important event like a demonstration, and I should have done something useful. But I didn't know what to do, so I couldn't help it. Then I saw Cindy Lou, and my face lit up and I waved to her. I shouldn't have done that, especially that thing with the light in my eyes. I know Mom hates it when my eyes get too lit up about anything that feels good to me but not so good to her. Quickly I checked if maybe I was lucky and she was too busy and didn't see. But she saw. She looked straight at me.

I know she will probably slap me later for it. But she will tell me it's for some other reason and also that it's for my own good. I'm not afraid or anything. She always does that when something makes her mad or disappointed. It doesn't hurt all that much. It just stings.

Still, I don't like it, so I tried to do something smart to maybe avoid it. "I'll go invite Cindy Lou to come stand with us," I offered. It seemed like a kind thing to do and I thought maybe it would impress Mom. "She's standing all alone over there."

"Don't you dare!" Mom snapped at me. There was real hatred in her eyes now. I just hoped it wasn't for me this time. Mom said this loud enough that some heads turned.

"But Mom, she's all alone."

Mom's voice softened, though it stayed loud enough for others to hear as well, and she started to explain. "She deserves to be all alone. She doesn't belong with us. She's against us."

I looked at Cindy Lou, careful not to have any excitement in my eyes this time, which was easy, since I really didn't feel any excitement anymore. Cindy Lou has curly short brown hair, sticking out in small tufts all around her head, and lots of freckles, big enough to see from a distance. She was wearing a pink sweatshirt and gray sweatpants that day, which made her look more comfortable than Mom who was wearing a suit with a narrow skirt. But Mom was definitely more elegant. Cindy Lou was holding a sign like everybody else. It said "WAR KILLS LIFE" and showed a big red and yellow flame explosion and black shapes blowing around in the air, but no people. Maybe it was better to imagine the people.

Our signs showed the usual little unborn babies in blood, or sometimes just in a beautiful baby curl still in a transparent mother sack.

I didn't want to ask any more questions, although I would have liked to know more. I'd always like to know more, but it's not possible. It makes Mom tired. It makes Daddy tired, too. So I usually have to leave things alone and hope for a day when I am sure they feel better and not so tired. Then I will ask. But by then I'll probably have so many questions, I will have forgotten half of them. I hope I'll remember the important ones.

I always knew Mom didn't like Cindy Lou too much, but I didn't realize that she thought Cindy Lou was an enemy. Mom doesn't like a whole lot of people, so it never meant all that much, I thought. Except Cindy Lou is the only person from our church whom Mom doesn't like. Mom said once, "She reminds me of Delia." Daddy said, "I don't see it," in the voice he uses when he is either embarrassed or doesn't want to talk about something.

I did ask him later, "Who is Delia, Daddy?" "Who?" he asked back, as though he didn't have a clue what I was talking about, but I think he did all along.

"Delia. Somebody called Delia. Mom said Cindy Lou reminded her of Delia."

"Oh," he said, turning pink, which he does a lot, and it's sort of cute. It always makes me want to protect him. "She's somebody I knew before your Mom and I got married. Someone we both knew," he corrected himself. "She must be much older now and probably looks nothing like Cindy Lou anymore."

That's all he would say.

So I imagine that Delia was the love of Dad's life, but somehow he got Mom pregnant and had to marry her, and now they're stuck with each other even though they sometimes don't like each other all that much. I know I'm not supposed to think those kinds of things. I'm supposed to be more innocent, which means I shouldn't know any of that sort of stuff. I'm pretty good at pretending that I know less than I do. And there are plenty of things, far too many, that I don't know for real. For example, sometimes Dad smells like Miss Spring, the organist, who always smells like spice and roses. I wonder if Mom notices that too. Men aren't supposed to smell like roses so much, but I guess they have to be pretty close to each other when they discuss the music for the next service.

Daddy doesn't come to the demonstrations. He says he can't do it to his parishioners to take sides. This makes Mom mad, too.

"But it's important," she told him once. "And if you don't go, you look like you're actually siding with the baby killers, don't you?"

He didn't say anything.

"So what is it? Are you really on their side? Do you think I should have gotten an abortion and Ellie shouldn't have been born? Is that what you think? And then you could have married that slut that you were so hot after? Is that it?"

"Honey, I won't discuss this in front of Ellie," he said. "She can hear you. Every word."

"But you won't discuss it anywhere else either," Mom said. "So I have to discuss it in front of her."

"That's right, I don't want to discuss it anywhere at all." Daddy turned away from Mom.

"Well, are you seeing her?" Mom asked. "Are you?"

He turned back and took a step toward Mom and kissed her on the forehead. I wish someone would kiss me that way some day.

"Does it hurt you with your congregation when I'm taking sides?" Mom asked, sounding much friendlier.

"It doesn't matter," he said. "Yes, it would be easier if you were less conspicuous. But far more important than that is that you do what you think is right." Now he kissed her on the top of her head because he's much taller than she is and she had her head bowed.

I don't mind you fighting in front of me, I wanted to tell them. Maybe I did mind a little because it can be scary. But it sounded like I could learn a lot when they were fighting, and I do want to know who they are and where I came from.

In one of her sunny moods, Mom once told me that I was the gift from God that made us a family, her and Daddy and me, and that we should always be grateful for that. I think that's nice. But most of the time she just reminds me that I should be grateful for being alive. Which I am. I wish I could show it better so that she would be convinced once and for all. I also wish I could be even more grateful. Maybe that will come.

"You wouldn't be here," Mom often explains to me. "Not if I had gotten an abortion like all those irresponsible women want to be free to do. Including, by the way, your fancy Cindy Lou."

Cindy Lou isn't mine, of course. But I do like her. For an adult, she's pretty awesome. She never talks down to me, and if I ask her a question, she always answers. But I better keep that to myself around Mom from now on. I really think Mom would prefer it if I hated Cindy Lou. At this particular demonstration, there were others like Mom, because everybody stayed clear of Cindy Lou, and some gave her dirty looks. But she just stood there and smiled. Sometimes she makes me think of Cinderella, but mostly because my name is Ellie, almost Ella, and that would make our names join.

I wished I had brought some peanuts so I could secretly drop them for the pigeons or the squirrels, whichever got there first. But of course I wouldn't have the guts to feed animals and birds while Mom and the others were doing serious things.

Finally Matt got here, too, which was a relief. At least I was no longer the only child. He's much better at this than I am, even though he's more than half a year younger. He's only just turned eleven. I wonder why he's so good at everything. He's beautiful, too. I also wonder whether his Mom tells him, too, that if it hadn't been for demonstrations like this, he wouldn't even be alive.

When she's around Matt's mother, Mrs. King, Mom sometimes pats me on the head and says, "She's my prize." But Matt is so much better at everything. Mrs. King doesn't even have to say anything for everybody to know who has the better prize. It isn't me.

Mom always says I should go talk to people on the street, like Matt does. But I can't. I'm too ashamed. Sometimes it gets pretty confusing. I am supposed to be ashamed about a lot of things, but when I am ashamed, then it's never the right time. I can't ever get things right.

Matt is a star. He stops people right on the sidewalk with his beautiful smile and his gray eyes and his golden curls. Of course I'm much too young, but if I weren't, I might fall in love with him. Maybe later. He shakes people's hands. Another part of me is jealous of him, though. Why can't I be that way? Why can't I make my Mom as proud of me as

Matt's mother is of him? But that's only natural, I guess. He's a boy. They're almost always better at everything.

We're in the same class at school, and we started out as really good friends. At first I had all the A's, though, and Matt had a few B's. But then my Mom told me not to be so proud, that nobody liked it when girls were smarter than boys. So I started making mistakes. Now Matt is better at school, too. But he's so nice and we both know that we are unplanned children. We have that in common.

But Matt was definitely wanted.

Me? I'm not so sure. Mom does say I'm a gift. Daddy and her got married when I was already on the way. So in a way I got Mom her husband. Only, I'm scared whenever they don't like each other or are mad at each other, though I don't really know what I have to be scared about. I'll never have to worry about a divorce because Dad is a minister, and ministers don't do that. I wonder why, when everybody else does. But that's how it is.

Suddenly I saw Matt go over to Cindy Lou. I wished immediately that I would have gone. Now he'd get all the credit, as usual. He started smiling at her, but he didn't offer to shake her hand, like he usually does with people. Which made sense because he knew her already. But suddenly his face changed and he no longer smiled. Cindy Lou kept smiling at him, though. He threw up his hands. Then he turned around and looked at his mother. Mrs. King looked very angry and went over to say something to Cindy Lou and then she pulled Matt away.

Now everybody seemed to hate Cindy Lou. I looked around and they all stared at her. I wished I could make it better for everybody. Look, I wanted to say, it's just Cindy

Lou from church. Matt's mother then sent over one of the two police officers who had been standing at the street corner all along. They have to do that, Mom says, when there's a demonstration. This police officer talked to Cindy Lou, and she kept smiling. So then he went to talk to Matt's Mom for a while. This time she looked angry with him.

I really wanted to do something. But I couldn't do anything. I'm only eleven. Which means I'm in a sort of prison. Someday I'll get out of that prison, I know. As long as I am in it, though, I do everything wrong. One time I did stand out front right on the sidewalk, and I tried to talk to a guy, like I am always supposed to. He laughed and said to me, "You're a bit young to want a baby already, aren't you? Otherwise I'd be happy to oblige." I turned back to look at my Mom, but she was busy talking to one of the other women. "I don't want a baby," I explained. "I just want other babies to have a right to be born." I don't think he understood what I was trying to say. "Well, I'll be looking for you in five, six years," he said with a little smirk that made me both ashamed and confused. I also knew it had been my fault somehow that he smirked because I couldn't explain things right. I always get things wrong somehow.

"Smile," my Mom suddenly said behind me, and I smiled quickly, though that's a problem, too. Once there was a picture of us in the local paper, and Mom looked great, but I looked awful. It's no use. I'm supposed to be grateful for being alive, but it isn't always easy.

I do like being alive, but sometimes I wonder, wouldn't it have been better if God had created me as a pigeon or a squirrel? They always seem to know what to do, and whatever they do, they never have to worry about committing a sin. They just move, bobbing their necks, or sliding around tree stems. Plus they don't always have to be grateful, though maybe squirrels and pigeons are grateful, too, and I simply don't know enough about it.

Part II:

At Home

THE LUCKY CHILDREN

I don't like to talk about it. A few times I did. I usually start like this: It wasn't really rape in the strictest sense of the word. In other words, I wasn't jumped at knifepoint in some alley. There was no force involved because I was drunk.

But he was in my bed in the morning. Not difficult, because we lived in the same house with a few other friends. When I woke up to find him next to me, my skin crawled. You see, I had never much liked him, though he did look a bit like Bob Dylan. He knew this.

I shook him awake. "What are you doing in my bed?"

"You were so cute last night," he said with puppy dog eyes.

"But I don't want you anywhere near me. You know that." He was sleeping around, bragging more than regretting that he needed treatment for VD from time to time.

"Yes," he said, now hanging his head. "I'm sorry."

He was good with children. I mean, really good, and with no creepy intentions in that regard at all. He could put them at ease like a magician. He made them happy, which was excellent as he was studying to be a pediatrician. By now he has probably saved several, if not many, children's lives.

I don't know if I could have ruined his career. Perhaps I was harsher on myself for my role in the scenario than a judge might have been. In any case, I never seriously considered turning him in. Recently I read the story of a girl getting a fellow student convicted for rape after she had voluntarily climbed in his bed for some cuddling. But she never agreed to the actual penetration he eventually wanted and accomplished, though they had had intercourse before.

At any rate, I never reported a thing. I didn't even tell our friends. Sometimes I am ashamed on behalf of the women in this world for not making my "no" count. And sometimes I am happy for the lucky children he has healed.

THE MISTAKES

Imagine the city touched by spring. An aging civilization has been under a spell for five thousand years. Still spring happens. The sun coaxes yellow crocuses from swollen buds; purple ones, too, and a handful of snowdrops on the edges of the dark top soil flower beds.

Two girls sit on the lowest step of five stairs leading up to a brownstone building. Their murmurs and giggles fill the air. Mandy wears her favorite red short-sleeved linen shirt over jeans. Scilla feels a thickness in her chest. She is jealous and sad. Her mother does not allow her to wear red because she is chubby. If she stays chubby and wears red, no man will ever marry her.

A pregnant young woman named Gerda waddles toward them, her face puckered with the discomfort of her heaviness.

"She's fat," Scilla whispers.

This surprises Mandy. True, the woman has a large belly, now that Scilla mentions it. Mandy hadn't noticed before.

"Tell her," Scilla urges, suspecting, correctly, that Mandy has no concept of pregnancy. Scilla has just recently learned about it from her older brother in hushed tones.

Mandy shakes her head. It feels too dicey, though it might not hurt the woman's feelings anyway. People always call Mandy skinny, and it doesn't bother her. It's just how she is. It bothers her mother, though. Once, as they were walking hand in hand, two boys behind them had made boisterous comments about her stick legs. Now Mandy has to wear two pairs of wool tights in winter to make her legs look bigger. Otherwise people might say her mother wasn't feeding her enough. Fortunately it is finally spring and legs are allowed to be what they are once again because nothing can be done about it.

"It'll be fun to tell her she's fat," Scilla says. "You'll see."

"You go ahead and tell her then," Mandy says.

"No. I thought of it. You have to do something around here to earn your keep. Okay, here she comes," Scilla prompts. "Now."

Meanwhile Mandy's mother, AnnaBeth, is washing dishes in her kitchen. The sun slants through the crystal pendant hanging in the window and paints faint rainbow patterns low on the wall. AnnaBeth doesn't notice. She is busy with her porcelain and the second best silver, and with her thoughts and her exhaustion. She feels frumpy after yesterday's run-in with her mother-in-law.

"Tom is *my* husband," AnnaBeth had stated in proud self-defense.

"A man can always get another wife. But he can only ever have one mother," her mother-in-law had countered with unassailable logic.

There's something about this motherhood mystique that bothers AnnaBeth all along. Not that you can put your finger on what the problem is exactly. Motherhood is always promised with such sunny colors as incredible fulfillment.

Honor is part of the promise, too. And joy. But that's not exactly what you get. You get embarrassed sex, a pleasure strictly for the entitled husband's benefit, and then you get condemned for it from the church pulpit while sitting in the pew smiling and wearing your best hat. After that you get the agony of delivery, aching breasts, maybe a photo taken from time to time, in which you smile even wider than in the church pew, and aside from that you get a lot of heartache and responsibility and a little bit of pride. But honor? Not in her experience.

You do get love, however. AnnaBeth loves her little daughter, her youngest child. Mandy is bright and times are changing. Perhaps it will be easier for her. AnnaBeth's sons are already older, almost beyond her influence.

Meanwhile two birds are chirping back and forth in the forsythia bush by the steps outside the building. No one notices, except perhaps some other birds at a distance. Pregnant Gerda has reached the two girls. The skinny one points at her with a shaky finger, grows beet red in her face and says, "You're fat, lady." The other girl, the chubby one, laughs.

This is the last straw.

"You'll hear about this," Gerda hisses at the skinny girl who looks at her with shocked and frightened brown eyes.

Without giving the brats another glance, Gerda lumbers past them and up the five stairs, breathing heavily, the laughter of the chubby one still ringing in her ears. She is twenty-two and feels like an old woman, a thousand years old. She has to get home and lie down.

Not that home is any great joy, with her mother administering the daily poison of contempt, which is, however, not nearly as hurtful as her elegantly white-haired father's avoidance of any eye contact and his endless pre-dinner prayers to his God in heaven who is far more important than any daughter on earth.

To placate both the father in heaven and the one on earth, Gerda is forced to pretend to be married to a worthy missionary currently in Ethiopia, and presumably destined to die from malaria in due course, or some other suitable ailment, which fictional marriage precludes, of course, any contact with any non-fictional real men, not that any of them would look at her twice, genetic plainness now compounded by the baby in her womb. Worse, it precludes contact with any women, too, for fear, her parents' fear, that she might spill the beans in a moment of vulnerability. With the result that she would cause shame and indignity to her parents, and, worst of all, to her parents' highly judgmental God.

Gerda is lonely. She wishes she had the strength to break away. Here comes her narrow-eyed mother.

"You've been rather a while," her mother says, suspicion exuding from her like a sharp scent. Gerda's nostrils flare. She doesn't know exactly why, but she tells her mother about the girl calling her fat. She wants to scream. She wishes she had somewhere else to go. But she is frightened and trapped. The refrain "so long as you live under our roof" drums through her throbbing head.

"I need to lie down," she says, avoiding further questioning. Her mother mutters something unfriendly behind her aching back before Gerda closes her door.

Meanwhile skinny Mandy, a bit troubled still about having let Scilla talk her into something she didn't want to do, has returned home. She is slightly bored.

AnnaBeth smiles at her daughter with warm brown eyes. Their eyes are like mirrors of one another. "Later you can come shopping with me," AnnaBeth says. "But I need to take a little nap first."

Mandy nods. Her mother does look tired. Mandy settles down at the kitchen table to cut out paper dolls from a clothing catalog. Something rattles against the window. For a moment, Mandy hopes for a secret magic message from someone, perhaps a fairy visitor, perhaps a little gnome with magic powers, perhaps even an enchanted fox. But when she looks up, it is, as usual, only the wind. Mandy sighs. She already has a stack of catalog paper dolls at least two inches thick. But there are always more pretty women with nice dresses and beautiful faces to cut out and add to her stack whenever a new catalog arrives and she is allowed to cut apart the old one.

AnnaBeth ruffles Mandy's hair and kisses the unruly brown curls on top of her daughter's bent head before she leaves the kitchen.

The doorbell rings. Mandy hears her mother talk, then another woman's voice. The voices are not happy and are getting less so. Mandy's mother is often not happy, and there is nothing Mandy can do about it. She knows. She has tried. Her best bet, therefore, is to tune out. Mandy sings to herself and starts cutting the outline of a smiling model in a billowing red dress.

Until her mother opens the kitchen door with a loud snap. AnnaBeth now looks like an ogre. Her face is blotched with red. Her cheeks are puffed out over thin lips and bared teeth. Her eyes are filled with anger. Everything in Mandy's body bristles and tells her to flee. But it is no use. There is nowhere to escape to.

Meanwhile two squirrels chase each other around the tree that reaches up to and beyond Gerda's second-story window. They spiral up. They spiral down. But Gerda doesn't notice. She lies flat on her back on the rickety bed in her old room. She wishes that damn child downstairs would stop screaming. She's hot enough as it is. With anger. With shame. With everything. It's probably one of the same kids that sat out front. First hurting her with their rude laughter and comment. Now making a ruckus. She wishes the horrible screaming would stop.

The pillow over her head doesn't help; it only makes things hotter. The screaming just keeps on coming, like a filthy wave. The bed meets each movement of her body with a different lump. Her body is heavy and hot. Too heavy to get up and do something about that brat.

Why must it be like this for her? She knows she must be grateful, even for her thin-lipped pious parents and their dance of her father's dominance with her mother acting as his faithful executioner, making it all happen according to his will. Gerda could be feeling this heavy and swollen and smelly and helpless elsewhere. Out on the street, for example, without shelter. Destitute.

"You can stay with us," her mother had said, speaking for both parents as always. "But if you do, you do it our way." Which means with the obligatory lies, so that her father continues to look good. So that God continues to look good. Everybody must look good. Gerda feels nauseous, not like the first weeks of her pregnancy, but now because she is heavy and afraid and there is no way out.

Gerda wishes she had a God to pray to, any gentle God instead of the stern one of her parents.

Meanwhile the sun is lovely outside, the singing of birds has picked up in the yard. The forsythia bush keeps bursting forth with yellow exuberance. A white cat sniffs the dark soil near it, contemplating chewing on something green.

Downstairs, inside, Mandy is screaming, having reached a sorrowful depth of despair. "Stop, Mom. Stop. Please stop."

It's all a mistake, but Mandy can't convince her mother who keeps hitting her with the old hand broom. And she won't stop. Even though it is a mistake.

It doesn't matter that it was Scilla's idea. That Mandy didn't want to insult the woman. Here comes the wood. No. Stop. Brown, gray, old, splintering hard wood.

Mandy screams that she will apologize to the woman. She doesn't know exactly why, but she will. Now is not the time to understand. Her mother has never hit her before. It must be a mistake. Nothing makes sense. Mandy has done things far worse without her mother beating her.

"Stop, Mom. I'm sorry. I'll tell her I'm sorry."

Why is her mother beating her? Perhaps she doesn't love her anymore. She has never beat Mandy before. Nobody has. Dad only beats boys. "Please stop." Mandy would do anything to stop the beating. There's blood on her skin. It frightens her. And still her mother doesn't stop. "Mom, please, please, please stop."

The only thing her mom has said is that she is ashamed of Mandy and that the woman upstairs is carrying a baby and that's why she now has to beat Mandy.

"Please stop. Mom. *Pleeease.*"

Meanwhile outside the sun is shining and inviting pleasure on anyone's bare skin, inviting blossoms to open, birds to carry sticks to their nests, white cats to stroll.

AnnaBeth has no thoughts, no compassion, no understanding, only unrelenting fury and a vague awareness of her misbehaved daughter's irritating screams. AnnaBeth moves like a machine. Lifting the broom and hitting her daughter's bare bottom, lifting and hitting. There is no more reason, no consciousness of all that makes up this merciless rage, only that the rage is there. It has swelled from a lifetime of being taught to be ashamed of being a woman, of compliantly knowing her place, of the effort of holding her nose just an inch above water, smiling, sitting in church, greeting people, knowing all the same she is despised, a handmaid, a cook, a cleaner, an organizer, and a receptacle for the husband's sexual needs, one who tractably keeps silent in church, just as the Bible commands.

Numbed by rage she dimly knows she has split from all sanity. One day she'll look back and be ashamed of this, too. The day I hit my daughter. But she cannot grasp it now. She is out of control.

It is a horror to her, her own daughter mocking a pregnant woman. She must teach the little miscreant that you do not mock a pregnant woman, a mother-to-be who should be held in the highest regard. You do not laugh at the fruit of sex.

Her rage is huge.

Meanwhile the spring day keeps unfolding blossom after blossom into a balmy mid-afternoon with no one the better for it. At long last Mandy is exhausted with screaming and begging and pleading. It feels as though her mother has beaten her for hours. Everything hurts, her throat from screaming; her chest from being unable to get her mother to stop; her bottom. The blood still frightens Mandy, though not too much. She's scraped her knees often enough. But that ugly gray hand broom keeps coming at her, over and over and over again. The worst now is the fear, though, that this will never stop and she will never be loved again.

"Please, dearest Momma. I'll never laugh again at anyone, at anything. I'll ask forgiveness. Forgive me, forgive me, forgive me. Please stop."

Mandy is good at asking for forgiveness. She has lots of practice, as she always has to ask for forgiveness from her father anyway. It usually works.

"Please forgive me."

She wishes her mother's face would be less frightening. That horrible wood, that horrible face.

"Forgive me. I love you, Mom. I'll do anything you want."

Her mother smells of soap, sweat, dust.

Meanwhile, up by the squirrels who still chase each other around the tree trunk near the second story window,

Gerda, beaded with perspiration, calls for her mother. Here she comes, thank God for that, even with her long-suffering face.

"Mother, could you please do something to stop that kid downstairs from screaming? I feel so sick and the screams are giving me a headache."

"Gerda, I can't and I won't. I just got back from their apartment telling that rude girl's mother how they had laughed at you, and now you want I should go over and stop the punishment? Make up your mind, and go yourself if you want."

Her face is mean.

Is that what Gerda hears, the child's punishment? She understands now. Her bed feels slimy with sweat. She should change the linens, but it's so much effort, and she can't ask her mother to do it for her.

"Okay, Mother," she hears herself say, but it isn't exactly she who is speaking, is it? It's her own useless corpse lying on this bed. Now she just wants her mother to go away. She wants the screams to stop. How long does she have to listen to them? Most of all she wants her mother to go away and leave her alone. She must think. She must do something.

It's safe here, except that she is so tired and her soul is dying.

What could she possibly do out there in the world? Would she really starve and be left to die, together with her baby, born or unborn, without help?

She revisits the dull fairy tale that has her married to a minister, someone like her father, a holy man. A far cry from the handsome guy she went clubbing with three times before he persuaded her to let him have sex with her in the back of his black hooded truck. Now she needs to keep up the fairy tale so that her father won't lose face. In front of whom exactly? Does God keep track of their puny little lives? Is it really all so important?

If she wants to save herself and her sanity, she'll have to leave. Does she have that kind of strength?

Suddenly she notices that the screaming has stopped. She can't quite remember when. There's quiet now. It feels like a blessing.

She is sorry now for the little girl downstairs.

And she is sorry for the sweet child in her body. That child is no shame. That child is a blessing. That child is life.

She will sleep now.

Tomorrow she needs strength.

Meanwhile, downstairs, AnnaBeth has fled into a migraine, and Mandy has fled into a corner of the living room, behind the potted rubber tree, waiting for love to resurface, almost convinced that eventually it will.

The spring blossoms that day will have blossomed almost in vain, and yet they are bursting forth with their relentlessly gorgeous zest, and roots and leaves stretch out with their eager tendrils of life. Imagine these tendrils of spring and of love burgeoning out. Perhaps someone will leave the city under its arid spell and find another way, or perhaps someone will come and teach something fresh. And then again, perhaps not. The crocuses are hopeful. The forsythia bush is hopeful, the snowdrops, the birds, the squirrels, the white cat. The sunbeams connect with life and lure everything into becoming juicy again.

Imagine.

THE FOOTNOTE

Usually Megan worked at the circulation desk. A student assistant had called in sick, though, and she shelved books while the head librarian himself had come out of his office to man the circulation desk.

"Would you have coffee with me one day?" A graduate student startled her from her shelving reveries. She flushed, having turned to him first with her most inviting can-I-help-you smile. He was not attractive. A burly face. He had nice eyes, though, brown, almost golden.

"Can't," she said. "I'm married."

"That's okay," he said. "I'm married, too. I still drink coffee, though."

She laughed.

She fixed pork chops for dinner. The blood seeped pink through the flour coating and made her wish they were vegetarians. Earlier she had ironed the bedroom curtains. It wasn't like her to do things like that and she didn't expect him to notice. It had given her a surprising jolt of satisfaction.

Ben, her husband, worked on the Sunday New York Times crossword puzzle, though it was Tuesday. He only had the lower righthand corner left to finish. In the background the TV murmured political debates. Ben was working on his dissertation. That was the main reason for the crossword puzzle, it elegantly avoided indices, tables of contents, and similar annoyances.

After dinner she reread a Georgette Heyer romance. She wondered how often she could reread it without becoming bored. She loved romances, but not the contemporary ones with their obligatory sex scenes.

"Fuck formatting," she heard from the dining room table, which doubled as desk. They had to be frugal on her library income and his scholarship stipend.

"Want me to take a look?" she asked.

"Yes, would you please?"

It took her most of two hours to get his dissertation cross-indexed and all the footnotes in their proper place, but it made her feel good. Worthy. A word that a Heyer heroine would have used with a disdainfully wrinkled nose.

Colin, the graduate student, sought her out at the circulation desk, ostensibly checking out a book.

"I still drink coffee," he said. "You?"

He looked a bit more put together than that day in the stacks. His smile was huge. He smelled of some kind of citrus cologne. Subtle.

"I do," she said. "But I'm still married."

"Yeah, me too. Aren't we the lucky ones? Here, I got something for you."

He slid a completed blue loyalty card from the Coffee Shack across the circulation desk.

"It's outside the cafeteria," he said.

"I know where it is."

She fixed meatloaf that night, Ben's favorite. She was tired and a bit cranky. He was as ever working on his dissertation. She watched him for a while. She loved his dark hair, long enough he could actually twirl a strand with his left hand. This was in bold defiance of his grandmother who scolded every time they visited and his hair was beyond military brevity.

"I did something wrong," he said.

"Do tell."

"With the damned formatting. I swear I don't know what I hit, but . . . ."

"Let me take a look."

It didn't take long to fix and was done before the meatloaf was ready to eat. Ben was good with YouTube, photos, and sundry apps, but not so much with word processing.

"Your dissertation is brilliant," she said. "One day I'll be proud to show up in your biography as your devoted wife."

"Yeah, as a footnote," he quipped. If she hadn't been so tired, it would have been funnier. As it was, she noticed the rank smell emanating from his sneakers by the front door. She might have to give them a rinse and apply some kind of deodorizer one of these days. He'd probably not get around to it.

"I took the liberty of bringing a picnic lunch to share," Colin said. He showed up at the library at 12:28 p.m., two minutes before she typically went out to lunch. His eyes were soft and brimming with admiration. Ben hadn't looked at her like that in ages. The way of the world and all that.

"I was going to have a pizza in the pub," she said. "Mushroom and green pepper. My favorite."

"We can get you a slice on the way up to the roof."

"The roof?"

"Yes. I have a key."

"I thought we're not supposed to go up there. How come you have a key?"

"That's a secret."

"But why?" She was flustered now.

"Because you are beautiful."

She knew if she went with him, she would eventually kiss him. It might not end with a kiss. She wished he were Ben, and she knew she shouldn't go. She loved Ben. But was this betrayal? All she wanted was some attention. Maybe one day when Ben's dissertation was done. Perhaps she should wait. And see. She was afraid there would be nothing to see.

"Hey, beautiful. Earth to Megan."

"What? Oh. I'm woolgathering."

"I know. Come on, let me sneak you up there, beautiful. Then I'll go get you your pizza. The view is really something. You can see the courthouse. And the river. The river is the best part."

"Okay," she said. "I mean, I don't need pizza if you already brought something."

"I even brought wine. But only plastic cups. It's a full moon, too."

"At lunch?"

"Well, you can't see it, but it'll officially be full at 1:07 p.m. I checked."

She craved innocence, but also his admiration. She felt pressure behind her eyes. He led her to the metal steps and, after making sure nobody was there to notice them, unlocked the metal door.

"Up you go," he said.

She stepped out into the sunlight. The view was amazing.

"Let's see what all I got here," he said.

She turned around. He held out a rose to her.

ECLIPSE

"For you," Alan said.

"Who?" Solveig frowned, put down her *Morte d'Arthur* and got up, not fast, to walk to his desk where he held out the phone to her. Wireless and cell phones were still something of the future. Alan knew she didn't like to talk on the phone. There was something threatening about phones. Why hadn't he done something? Told whoever it was she had flown to the moon, for instance? Books were easier. The only good thing was that, usually, nobody called her in the first place.

"Don't know," Alan said in answer to her question. "Some guy."

She took the receiver still frowning. "This is Solveig Silverwell," she said with an inquisitive upswing of invitation.

"Dean Hammer from Stanford University," said a booming, friendly voice. She felt a jolt. "I have with me Boswell Goldfarb from the Goldfarb Foundation. We have good news for you. We're calling to let you know that you've been selected as one of this year's three recipients of a Goldfarb Foundation Fellowship."

Solveig caught her breath. "Really?" she said, already regretting her helpless inelegance.

"Really," Dean Hammer confirmed to her, his voice touching her like vibrations of a kettle drum. "Our committee met today to select the final candidates. We wanted to let you know right away."

"Wow," she said, feeling foolish. "Thank you." She felt heat crawl into her face, touching her skin with fine fire. She was also aware of Alan a few feet away from her, he being the reason for not shouting madly with jubilation.

"You'll receive your official notification in the mail in a few days. We hope you will be able to let us know within the next three weeks whether you want to accept your appointment as a Goldfarb Foundation Fellow."

"Yes," she whispered. "I will. Thank you for calling, Mr. Hammer, Mr. Goldfarb. I feel so honored. Thank you so much."

"Our pleasure, Ms. Silverwell."

Solveig still felt fire under her skin as she put down the receiver. "Yes!" she whispered in contained celebration.

She knew Alan had listened to every word of her side of the conversation, which was one of the reasons she hated the phone. Someone could always hear your end of the conversation, even when you turned your back to them.

"What was that all about?" Alan asked, curiosity all over his face, mixed with suspicion.

"Some dean from Stanford," Solveig said. Her heart still hammered with pleasure at the unexpected offer. True, she had applied; true, she had good grades. But the University of Minnesota, where Alan was now in his first year of graduate studies with a fellowship of his own, had not accepted her at all.

"They accepted me at Stanford," she said.

"That's nice," Alan said. "I guess."

"And they're offering me a fellowship."

"Oh," Alan said. He in turn had not been accepted at Stanford to continue after his completed Master's Degree, so he would have to stay at the University of Minnesota for his doctorate.

Solveig's head was spinning. It was possible, wasn't it? So they'd study in different parts of the country. They were still married. They were still companions for life. She still loved him, and she always would.

"So, are you going to . . . go?" Alan asked cautiously.

"Yes," Solveig said, equally cautiously. She touched her burning cheeks with fluttering fingers. She looked into his beautiful gray eyes and found them full of pain. She looked away.

"I see," he said.

He didn't bring up the discussions they had had that, if they didn't get into the same schools, it would be her turn to support the relationship for a while wherever he went to school. But this was different surely? A full scholarship with living expenses? They had never discussed that as an eventuality because neither of them had expected it. Especially not after her painful interview with one scholarship outfit where she was asked numerous times what impact her being married would have on her career. She had not received an offer for that scholarship.

"Congratulations, by the way," Alan said when they went to bed that night. "You've done well. I didn't say much before, I know. I guess it came sort of as a surprise."

"Thanks," she said. She felt warm in his arms and, for the first time, genuinely proud.

She graduated eighth in her class in college. Three years earlier, Alan had graduated ninth in his class. He was the one who brought it up. It wouldn't have occurred to her otherwise.

In the summer he went to Stanford with her to find a place for her to live. Both of them were scared. He feared for her safety, a young woman in the world on her own, though the surroundings, Palo Alto, turned out to be reassuringly university-dominated. She in turn was scared that, if she didn't find a suitable place, she'd be forced to abandon her plans. Secretly she also already looked forward to spending her spare time exploring nearby San Francisco. She was so excited about starting an academic life all of her own.

They returned to Minnesota until it was time for her to move. "Just for when school is in session," she reminded him. "It'll be three years at the most. And if you're done with all your course work before then, you can come and write your dissertation in California. We'll be together again."

He was studying history. She was planning to get her PhD in medieval literature, with emphasis on French or German, she hadn't decided yet. She already dreamt of spending quality time with Tristan and Ysolde, King Arthur, Parzival, and whoever else might show up. And to think that she would even get paid for it.

Being a medieval scholar wasn't a very practical career choice, even for academia, but there was ample precedent of people making a living by conducting scholarship. She planned on being brilliant.

Alan's academic specialty was World War I and World War II and the American experience in between. Perhaps his choice of study was a bit more practical.

While back in Minnesota for the summer, they gave a dinner for Alan's best friend, Ned, and Ned's wife, Andy. Ned was a history scholar like Alan, but two years ahead of Alan because he had lucked out of the draft. He had just nabbed a teaching position at a small college in Minnesota. His wife Andy worked as a computer specialist with punch cards at a time when computers were still a rarity and personal computers not yet on the market.

For one last time Solveig and Alan sat in their cozy one-bedroom garden apartment entertaining guests. It was summer, lovely, with the windows open and the bugs screened out. In honor of the occasion, they had bought slightly more expensive wine than usual.

After she moved to California, Alan would give up the apartment and move into a group house to save on rent, and she already had her efficiency apartment lined up near the university. Unlike Alan, she didn't like shared living quarters. For Solveig, living with a husband was challenging enough, and her absolute limit. "Hermit at heart," Alan had called her once.

Andy and Alan paired up in conversation and seemed to be happy with each other. For a while Solveig watched them while clearing the table. She envied their comfortable cheerfulness, wishing she could be part of it somehow. However, she had never quite connected with Andy, who, for no particularly good reason, always seemed to look down on Solveig.

Unfortunately this left Solveig, after the dishes were cleared and nothing more could possibly be done to keep her busy, to make at least an effort at conversation with Ned, not a particularly attractive prospect. For one thing, Ned was decidedly not in favor of women and their so-called liberation. He seemed convinced, and typically quite vociferously so, that women's ability to think or do anything else particularly useful was limited at best. She'd previously been a bristling witness to conversations between Alan and Ned, in which women were summarily declared inferior in mathematics for certain, and many other types of thinking besides. Alan would wink at her now and again reassuringly, but still seemed to enjoy the slam-the-ladies conversation enough to not put a stop to it in response to her pleading entreaties with her eyes. How Andy could comfortably be married to Ned was beyond her.

"Why do you hang with this guy," Solveig had asked Alan once.

"Because he's my friend."

True to form, friend Ned now slithered into judgment about her imminent move to Stanford.

"Do you really think you're doing the right thing?" he asked, leaning forward into her space.

"Yeah," she said, leaning back. "It's a fantastic opportunity. They're paying for everything."

"Alan tells me your scholarship stipend is more than his."

"Well, yeah. It's California versus Minnesota. Cost of living is much higher out there."

Ned was handsome. Long dark eyelashes softened his lazy eyes. "Don't you think you are hurting Alan by competing with him?" he asked.

Solveig's muscles contracted. She felt heat flood her cheeks. Quickly she looked to see if Alan or Andy were listening. They were not.

"No," she said, her arms circling a defensive gesture. "I'm not competing with him at all. I'm just doing what I do well."

"You don't think it hurts him to have you do better than he is doing?"

"I'm not doing anything better."

"Graduating eighth in your class to his ninth?"

"He told you that?" Solveig was embarrassed.

"Obviously made an impression on him." Ned's eyes were intense slits for a moment. He seemed to enjoy himself. When his eyes widened again, he looked like a righteous evangelist sure of eventual triumph. You might be a lowly sinner, Ned's eyes said, but you could still be saved, and here am I, willing to show you the way.

Solveig shuddered. "He was just kidding!" she said with pretended confidence. Because Alan had mentioned it to her as well, she now felt insecure. Her class had been larger than his, too—she had already checked it out, just in case his class had been the larger one and she could have cited that in his favor as a peace offering to his ego. But it wasn't the case.

"What do you think it makes him feel like to have you outdo him?" Ned asked again, his soft and subtly hateful eyes resting on her. Hateful to whom? He was just protecting his friend. She knew that.

"Well, Ned, I know he doesn't want me to sit around like his mother, knitting and watching TV and reading romances and mysteries."

"How do you know?" Ned asked. "Maybe that's exactly what he would like."

Solveig was exasperated. Ned didn't know a thing. "He's proud of me," she said.

Ned raised his wine glass. "Drink to that?" he said.

"Sure," Solveig said, heat licking the inside of her chest.

"What are you two toasting?" Alan asked when their glasses clinked.

"Your wife's success," Ned declared.

"And yours," Solveig added quickly. "And Andy's. And Ned's."

"I'll drink to that," Alan said. "Andy?"

Andy's glass was empty and Alan filled it for her.

"Still, Robert Graves is right, you know," Ned said. "Women are goddesses and muses. As such they inspire us. Muses are always female. There's no one around to inspire women, not like they inspire men anyway." He smiled at Andy and Solveig in turn. The two women just stared at him.

Alan took Solveig to the airport.

They had made love the night before, she with a sense of owing him, he with a need to claim her body, claim her sex. She wanted to be more devoted to him physically, but she couldn't focus on him at all. It was as though her body was already miles away on her own quest. He didn't seem to notice.

There was construction at the airport, and she had to go through a pedestrian particle board tunnel to get to her gate after they had hugged their last hug and kissed their last kiss. She turned around several times to wave.

"I love you," she mouthed with tears in her eyes and excitement bubbling in her heart.

Alan looked lonely against the sky blue and rust background of the airport walls and carpeting. His lips were pressed into a benevolent smile under his blond moustache. She couldn't see his eyes, which was just as well. He raised his right hand and waved.

Alan came to visit her for Thanksgiving. She was glad, though she had a lot of reading to do. It could wait for a few days, and she'd get in some late at night when Alan was already sleeping.

Solveig hadn't made any friends; well, one, but she was a crazy lesbian, and the crazy part was not that she preferred women to men, but that she wanted to watch endless surrealistic movies for recreation. Solveig preferred to stay at home and read. She treasured her solitude. But she knew she was expected to feel at least a little lonely, so it was a good thing Alan came.

They both went to Alan's parents' place for an extended family Christmas.

Solveig sent Alan tulips for Valentine's day since roses were no longer available at the last minute when she happened to remember. He called to thank her for the roses. She was shocked at how little notice he took of reality.

Her school work went well. She finished her first semester with straight A's, which she by now more or less expected, so no great cause for excitement. Alan called a few times to report that he was floundering, listless, couldn't get a grip on himself to settle down to his studies, had lost momentum somehow. He said he missed her, but insisted it was no big deal. Since she was celibate in her California setting, and so intent on finishing her studies as quickly as possible that she hardly noticed her surroundings, much less any young men navigating through the same classes she attended, it didn't even occur to her that he might fall in love with someone else back in Minnesota. Her earlier ambitions to take time to explore San Francisco in her spare time made her laugh now. That mythical spare time simply didn't exist. Her main entertainment aside from her studies consisted of inhaling the scents of a dozen sample vials of perfumes she had purchased from an ad in the Sunday paper.

As spring unfolded, at least in California, Alan called her less often rather than more, though he did tell her each time that he missed her. One time she thought she heard tears clogging his throat, but it was probably only her imagination. She missed him, too, missed having someone to whom she belonged in the quiet evenings in her tiny square of a home where almost every inch was covered with papers. She felt guilty for having left him to flounder by himself back home in Minnesota, where it was still cold and dreadful.

She continued to be inept on the telephone and never felt she had much to say. One day, though, they had an odd kind of argument during their call, she couldn't afterwards remember what about, and at the end of it Alan poignantly said, "Ned says to say hello."

That night she got drunk on very cheap beer. She didn't want to face things anymore. For a moment, it felt cute to have the bed spin around her after she had finished the six pack, sort of like the bed in the Perilous Castle, though there were no swords over her bed to dodge.

Nobody believed, it appeared, that she wasn't competing with her husband. In fact, nobody took much interest in her at all, neither the professors, nor her fellow students, and when they did, it was by way of raised eyebrows when she mentioned that, yes, she was married and her husband was working on his own PhD back home in Minnesota. They simply didn't know what to do besides raise eyebrows and change the subject.

When she told her favorite professor that she considered not coming back in the fall, he didn't say one word of regret. That hurt. Maybe her brilliant academic career wasn't going all that brilliantly. Her lesbian friend didn't express much in the way of regrets either. Solveig was of no importance here at all. It wounded her, just as the thorny guilt at choosing her own life over contentedly playing second fiddle to Alan's life wounded her. How on earth were they going to find a job in a reasonably convenient place where they could actually live together, when they couldn't even manage to get into the same university for graduate school?

For a rarity, she called Alan on her own initiative to tell him that she was going to come back to Minnesota for keeps.

"Don't do anything drastic on my account," he said half-jokingly.

But it was all on his account, she thought, including her quest for academic recognition. She wanted him to be proud of her. "Of course not," she said.

She went to the campus counselor, but once there, she couldn't explain what her problem was. Maybe there wasn't a problem. Maybe she was merely abandoning a career that might not have suited her anyway.

She took a train back home to be able to slow down the distance between her past and her future. She didn't know yet what to call her new path. Defeat? Devotion?

Alan still lived in the group house, and she was uncomfortable about joining him there as a guest, but it wasn't going to be for long. She mostly withdrew to Alan's room, which she never quite considered theirs, rather than mingling in the common living room area, cozy though it was.

One day, looking for a pencil sharpener, she found some gold-threaded pony tail holders in his desk drawer. "Where did you get those?" she asked. "Planning to let your hair grow?"

"No." Alan blushed. "They probably belong to Lisette. She's somebody who came to visit Richard in the spring, and I let her stay in my room."

Solveig tried her best not to blush in turn at her own stupidity of asking. Now he probably thought she was snooping, and it wasn't even the mere idea of him potentially having an affair that hurt so much, but the embarrassment of him thinking of her as being jealous or suspicious or feeling humiliated in any way.

Sometimes she drank a glass of wine or two at night to help her go to sleep. She liked wine much better than beer, despite the interesting spinning bed experience in California. After they moved into an apartment of their own again, she drank every night. She didn't quite know why. It wasn't as though she really needed to. It just felt pleasant. It also rubbed out some of the guilt she felt. Now the guilt was about having abandoned a promising career for a man, where earlier it had been about abandoning a man who needed her for a mere career. Whatever she did, she was going to be hounded by guilt one way or the other. Wine made her lose focus, which felt good.

For all her belated loyalty, she lost Alan in due course anyway. There came a time when she did not want to burden him with her personal dissatisfaction and self-pity anymore. After some time Alan accused her of being weak for throwing in the towel rather than fighting for her own existence. For his part, when she rejoined him, his own lassitude did lift and he finished his graduate studies brilliantly. There was always also the nagging suspicion that Alan did after all prefer to live with a pliable lush rather than a productive human being. To have to put up with a lush was perhaps more acceptable than to have an equal for a wife. She was afraid of being labeled either a masochist or a castrating bitch. It seemed as though there really was no viable middle ground.

After Solveig left him, Alan went to Indonesia. "Had to go somewhere, do something," he would say later. "Was shook up." He helped, among other things, with setting up a school for girls of the not so wealthy echelon to rival the Catholic schools where their wealthier peers were allowed to pursue learning. At least he did something for women, Solveig thought.

Their divorce became final when Alan was still in Indonesia. He came back after a few years, due to an illness he couldn't shake, with a lovely new wife, Merpati. Yes, lovely was the word for her. She was a bright and beautiful young woman devoid of all ambition for herself. She, unlike Solveig, had been able to skip the phase of numbness and self-avoidance through drinking, and had moved straight from being a brilliant young lady to being a reader of mysteries and romances and a decorator of the home and an arranger of flowers. She knew how to entertain guests. She had come from the wealthier Catholic school background rather than the school that Alan had helped get off the ground. But one wasn't supposed to be prejudiced. So Alan ended up married to the kind of woman Solveig had once hoped to become. Lovely and spiritual. And beloved.

Would it have been better, Solveig sometimes mused, to just plod along without high hopes in the beginning? Like they say, servants who know their place and have no hope of jumping status are the happiest. Maybe that's all that women were good for, after all, mulch for men's growth.

In her dreams Alan would speak into a microphone: 'Yes, I loved her', he would say. 'I was afraid of losing her. She was beautiful, I thought, and smart, and I'd be a few thousand miles away. True, she was shy. But would she stay that shy without me around to keep an eye on her?'

Ned would stand beside Alan in her dreams, and add: 'Oh, yeah, I remember her. She was a blond little fluff, pretending to be an intellectual. With a name like Solveig, she should have stayed in Minnesota all along.'

One thing about drinking heavily was that it gave Solveig access to some of her anger, which in sober reality was out of the question. When drinking, she realized how wounded she was, not with people actively hurting her—but with people not supporting her chance to grow fruitfully into who she had always imagined she was destined to become.

Solveig floundered in respectable administrative jobs. Sometimes she had bursts of ambition, but only once, quite early on, did a prospective employer ask her why she was applying for a secretarial job with her academic background and potential. Through the years she drank a lot of alcohol for a variety of reasons. She drank red wine for its sheer beauty, though it sometimes gave her a bit of a headache. Food coloring did that, she learned in time. When the headaches got too frequent, she would switch to white wine for a while. She went through a phase of peach wine, too, which was delicious, then plum wine. She even tried mead, which would have gone well with her former medieval studies.

During phases of drinking she sometimes remembered the first round of defeat, asking her older brother to take her along on a trip to the Grand Canyon.

"No, you're a girl." Then came his kindly afterthought. "Besides, you're too young."

As frequently happened with young girls, Solveig had started out more successful at school than her brother Gunnar. Her SATs and GRTs were top notch. His had to be padded with personal salesmanship at various deans of admissions' offices. He had plodded through college, then a master's, then a PhD, and was now teaching business administration at a junior college.

Alan, with whom she stayed in touch loosely, reported to her that Ned had taken to cocaine and couldn't hold a job because he didn't treat his students with enough business-like forbearance. He considered himself old school, believing that students shouldn't get away with receiving a degree just because they paid for it. Still yet, the students and their tuition money were necessary to the college. So said the administration. Finally Ned was fired for running into problems with his female department head.

Andy supported Ned with her computer work, and she despised him. She had affairs that never quite satisfied her, including a brief one with Alan. So everyone had found their niche. Including Solveig, watching the reflection of light in the jewel-red wine in her glass.

Sometimes she glided deep into acceptance of her lot, which always felt a little bit like death. At other times, in her dreams and forgetfulness, she still saw herself as capable of somehow making an important contribution with her life.

Anyway, nobody was waiting for her spectacular contribution to the world. Nothing was holding its breath for her. Only she held her breath as she dragged her heavy shell of a body through her days, more often than not blessed by the beauty of a tree branch laden with wind-blown icicles, or the sun glistening on water. There was always some extraordinary beauty caressing her. Sometimes, in her dreams, she had the courage to give herself to the world with all her unbridled talent. And once she dreamt she was a red leaf laughing down a waterfall.

THE GIRL WHO MOVED TO

ATLANTA

Megan lifted the second to last of the remaining boxes into the trunk of her Mazda; three boxes, if you counted the small box of jewels. Her cell phone rang. "You'll like it in Atlanta," she remembered her friend Denise telling her. She would stay with Denise until she got her footing.

She punched the green call button on her phone.

"I've finally finished my paper on 'To Room 19'—can I bring it to you?" That was Elyse, one of Megan's problem students, brilliant, talented, and lazy.

Former students, Megan corrected herself silently. "You'll have to send it to me. I'm moving to Atlanta," she said, trying to keep the thickness of tears out of her voice.

"Can I just leave it in your inbox for next semester? I don't mind an incomplete. I'm not graduating yet."

"No, you'll have to send it to me. I'm not coming back."

"What?" A gratifying shriek from Elyse.

"Let me give you the address," Megan said.

"Say it isn't so!" Elyse wailed. "You're my favorite professor. I want to take something from you every semester!"

"Sorry."

"Well, where are you teaching in Atlanta, then? Maybe I can transfer?"

Megan laughed. She didn't have a job in Atlanta yet. Nothing lined up, nothing in the works. An image of receiving her doctoral cap shimmered before her as she closed her eyes. The autumn scent of juniper and cedar of her first day of classes as assistant professor.

"....dark though," Elyse's voice brought her back mid-sentence of enthusiastic babbling. "The woman committing suicide and masking it as politely as possible, so it doesn't hurt the husband and the children. That's so real."

"To Room 19" had been the most controversial story she had taught in her Composition I class. Half of the students had been upset by the stealthy truth of the story. Could have happened. Here. Now. The other half were upset the other way around, claiming it couldn't possibly be true.

"It's so not PC. It portrays women as weak. And Doris Lessing was supposed to be a feminist?"

"Actually, the feminists claimed her, but she always claimed she wasn't one. She wanted to be a humanist, not a feminist. She wanted to show the truth as she saw it, not according to some theory or philosophy, but according to reality."

"Reality, shmality," someone had muttered.

"Well, may I bring you my paper before you leave?" Elyse asked, pulling Megan back to the present.

Megan briefly considered waiting, but, no, that part of her life was over. For now. "I'm leaving in ten minutes," she said.

"Oh. Then you better give me your address."

All her life people had warned her about studying English literature, which she loved. "You'll never find a job with an English major." It was worse when she went on to graduate school. "Come on, Megan, you'll be teaching Composition 101 and Intro to Literature for the next ten, twenty years."

She had in fact taught Composition and Introduction to Literature. She didn't mind. Both lent themselves to smuggling in her favorite women writers, with the additional small triumph of getting to require young men to read women authors, too. Easy with someone like Mary Oliver, of course, whom practically everybody embraced. Another one who declared herself as not being a feminist.

What did get Megan to abandon her academic career for the time being was of course, of all things, a man.

"It's always about a man, isn't it?" shrieked the collective furies in her mind.

Shawn was a colleague who had been hired two years before her, and Shawn was a hero.

Each English student took one class with Shawn. Some might have taken more, but it was painful to listen to him. It was easier by far to look at him. His face was movie star handsome with large brown eyes, long lashes, lush brown hair, a carefully trimmed beard.

He always held his head to the side, and it wasn't until he spoke that one could tell that there was something wrong. His vocal chords often snapped out of control, a modulated phrase or two, then a sudden dark derailing, a clang, a metallic squeak. That's when one started noticing that half of his suit seemed oddly loose.

Shawn had wanted to be an English Professor, much as Megan had, and he had succeeded against all normal odds—and then some, in his case.

When in her third year of teaching Megan proposed a class of Women and Literature from the 20th Century to the present, Shawn had joked that he would teach Men and Literature from 3,600 B.C. to the present.

Shawn was popular. Yes, he was in a wheelchair and all doors opened for him. At faculty parties, he was surrounded by well-wishers.

At first Shawn and Megan didn't have a lot to do with one another.

One day he published a book of poems with a university press. The English faculty organized a poetry reading for him. Each of five teachers was to take turns reading one poem after another, standing by the side of Shawn's wheelchair. Due to his voice challenges, he would not read.

Not many students were expected, but many came. Extra chairs had to be brought in.

By the day of the event, three teachers had canceled, however, leaving only Megan and an older professor, close to retirement, who thought perhaps it would be better for her to do the entire reading.

She did so. On a few occasions she had tears in her eyes. Shawn was openly weeping. The students gave a rousing applause.

That was when Shawn fell in love with her.

Shawn asked Megan out for coffee, but she declined. He frightened her with his intensity and she kept avoiding him as much as she could.

He wrote her a letter about the poetry reading. How many students had commented on what a stunning pair they made, what an amazing team.

The students had told her that as well.

One day he wheeled to her office door in his wheelchair, which blocked it so effectively that she couldn't have escaped, even if she had gone for the absolute in soap opera and run away.

"Why are you avoiding me?" he asked.

"I'm not," she lied. She thought of the beggar in front of the Lutheran church whose morning hello made her feel obligated and made her opt for slinking through an unpleasant alley instead.

"I've written you two letters, eight notes, and fourteen emails. You haven't responded," he said.

"I haven't had time. I have so many papers to mark."

He looked as bitter as some of his poems. He had good reason to be full of rage at life. She conceded him that. But it scared her.

"You're avoiding me because I'm crippled," he said. His dark eyes flashed hatred.

Blood rushed into her nerve endings. She was trapped in truth.

"Shawn, I like you well enough. You know that."

"Then prove it. Go out for a coffee with me. It's just coffee."

"Thank you, Shawn, but, no, thank you for asking. I can't."

"Why?"

"Because . . . ."

"No reason, right?"

Oh, there was a reason. He was pressuring her. It alarmed her. But one couldn't say such a thing. Well, maybe someone else could have, but she personally could not.

She went out for coffee with him. Later he would accuse her, "You went out for coffee with me. You encouraged me."

The next week he turned up everything a notch. This time he wanted to go out to dinner. She didn't. They went to dinner. He smiled. His eyes no longer hated her.

Later he would say, "You just wanted to be chased."

And in the night she was visited by demons that taunted her. What harm does it do to go out with him? You are a good girl, aren't you? It was to avoid her inner demons more than anything else that made her pack and leave.

In the car, driving south, then east, away from the sunset, she cried. For herself. For her students growing up into a society where you could still be forced. For Shawn and his belief that the world owed him whatever he wanted.

"Just call me the girl who moved to Atlanta," she sobbed into her steering wheel. "No, not girl, I'm a woman," she corrected herself a moment later. "A woman who does what needs to be done." Her demons were milder in daylight. They merely asked why she didn't stay and fight for her space. Because she was a woman who knew that any space gained in fight, anything drenched in conflict and in pain, was not worth living in, she replied. Because it was dangerous to hurt a wounded man's feelings in this world. It was easier to move to Atlanta than to keep on saying no.

She had a lot to learn from him, she thought, as a cloudburst made her slow down and turn on the windshield wipers to full speed. How to overcome weakness. And how to use it to advantage if necessary.

Perhaps her friend Denise was right. Perhaps she would like it in Atlanta.

Shawn wheeled into the staff lounge where the new teacher, red-haired Karina Alkhinoff, sat reading a copy of his book of poems he had recently given to her.

"I hear a former colleague of yours gave a legendary reading of these poems," Karina said, looking up.

"Yes," Shawn said, dream lights wandering into his eyes. "I still miss her. She was a fine woman. We were a great match. Unfortunately she had to move. One of her parents was ill—her mother, I believe. If I had asked her to stay, I think she would have stayed. But it would have torn her apart inside. I couldn't ask such a thing of her. I cared too much."

Karina loved the velvet sincerity in Shawn's eyes.

FOURTEEN DAYS IN NOVEMBER

First day of November

Up in the morning with a shiver of faint fear. Doesn't matter. Nothing matters. I'm prepared for the whole kaleidoscope of living, every strand of color, be it blood or blue veins in the clouds.

I accept the mistakes, too. They bind us to the network of strange faces and unresponsive eyes. I haven't really lost anyone who matters to me by coming to this strange country, this tiny village. I need my solitude to paint, and solitude has welcomed me. Though all the folks in the village know me by now. Or about me at least. Sometimes they go a few steps out of their way to say hello. Even just to look at me. A woman, alone and barely twenty-two, come to their unremarkable village—happens to be cheap to live in—to do nothing but sketch and paint all day and write letters or read books at night. I wonder what they think.

Two days ago I met an old man in the street. He tottered, from early afternoon ale rather than age, and started rambling about his enemies and friends. I qualified as friend. Before he finally walked on, he shook both my hands and said, "You're a lovely girl. Take good care of yourself."

In other words, don't get in trouble.

I wonder what he and the rest of them would think if they knew.

There's nothing to know, of course. That's right, nothing. Except that I'm here to gather colors and shapes to bring back home with me. Strange to think of home at a time like this. Night wind swishes around the edges of the house. My windows face west. I look to the dark west where all my friends are now. Names, faces, memories, and whispers of the past. All vague. Loose ends. Becoming slack.

So I lose myself in fantasies. Finding, for instance, a small child of my own. Some tiny angel I could live with effortlessly. Someone who would never leave me.

The fantasies expand. With a small fatherless daughter I might finally become the rebel and the outcast I was always meant to be. Scorned, celebrated, feared. Subject to all the attitudes they have toward someone they don't know what to do with.

I wonder whether anyone will ever understand my innocence.

Second day of November

Sweet Jesus, I'm afraid.

I'm not a star fallen from heaven. I'm just like everyone else. And now afraid. The mirror copies my face same as always. Why doesn't it crack? Yes, there were others in this situation before me. Then why am I so utterly alone?

Couldn't paint today. I took the easel to the shore by the red-blooming fuchsia shrubs. The sky was the most amazing deep green. Yes, green. I cursed it. Like a child that hates a beautiful toy it doesn't know how to play with. Like a child who knows that even the ugliest words can always only thinly hide the unbearable weeping inside.

Like a child. Oh, child, must you already intrude into the pompous constructs of my mind? Must you teach me already how much you are there, and how low I have fallen?

Can words be as bitter as the knowledge I have? Let me try.

Seven weeks ago James flirted with me across the table at a dance. Six weeks ago he came to take me out for a drink. We had seven a piece. That is, I had seven. He may have had more. He drove me home and stopped by the road. He said he was a virgin. I laughed. And then he ploughed into my body with all the vehemence of wounded pride. Three weeks ago I missed my period. Two weeks ago we met once more. I meant to talk to him about my fears. Instead we parted quickly, after saying nothing, and that with mutual contempt.

I scrubbed myself for hours. Bought vinegar for douching. I imagined it burning my delicate skin. I stretched, I knelt, I squeezed my belly with my fists. How could a soul choose to take root in a small body so uninviting?

Instead of talking to James, I drove him away. Could he smell the fear on me with the sure instinct of a guilty party who already hears potential allegations in the timid silences of the accuser?

Third day of November

Tonight I sat in the deep chair by the fire, reading. From time to time I looked into its light. Blue flames, red flames, and smoke. When I stood up, there was a leap in my stomach, a carnival ride feeling. I nearly passed out. I held on to the back of the chair and stared in the mirror. Am I truly pregnant then? No answer of course, except the gray smudges of my fear staring back at me.

Could be the smoke from the fireplace that makes me faint like this. The sweetness of turf burning. I wish I had something strong to drink. I'm trying to listen to the inside of my body. Can't hear a thing.

I won't put new turf on the fire, though the bucket is still nearly full. Better to watch the fire than to watch myself, even as I let the fire die. Tiny flames dart through the black hollow of the hearth, like devil's eyes. I seek forgiveness where there is none.

It's all right, it's all right. Spit at me then, if you must.

Fourth day of November

I walked the seven miles to town today. Got to have something to read. Mrs. O'Neil doesn't have anything except the Bible and a four hundred page Stephen King paperback with a lurid cover. Drops of blood slashing through geometric shapes of black and white.

I spent nearly an hour in the supermarket, relishing the anonymity and selecting, finally, three paperbacks. There's a book of local fairy tales I'd like to get before I leave this place. But it costs a lot. It can wait. At least until I know how my money will hold up.

On the way back the sky was overcast. Two miles down the road I got caught in torrents of November rain. I stopped for shelter in the small store where the road to the village forks off. Too shy, for some reason, to ask for something warm to drink, I bought a carton of milk. When the rain let up, I went on, hoping for a ride for part of the way like the last time I came back from town. But it was early afternoon and not another soul on the road.

I passed the odd brick house of the old man who always calls off his two fierce dogs just barely before I pass the fence. As usual he greeted me. "It's wet to be walking out today," he said. True, it was drizzling again just then. But there he was, outside himself, undaunted, puttering around in his brown November garden.

Then came the part of the road I wanted to pass quickly. I didn't even want to look. But I did look, as though compelled by some evil spell. It's just a triangle of leveled ground, cut straight into the gentle hillside, marked by three huge boulders. The sand is covered with lorry tracks, a few car tracks. The freshest tracks were from a car whose driver must have changed his mind and used this spot to make an almost perfect half-circle back to the direction where he had come from. Soon the rain will wash all tracks away.

And that's where James pulled the car off the road, announcing that he had to take a leak and that he was a virgin. And that's where I laughed too loud to prove God knows what, and that's where he kissed me with hideous challenge and I kissed back with drunk defiance. That's where I saw his blurred, angry grin, and where he pulled my pants off and leaked straight into me. That's where I ached for tenderness and felt instead something far closer to embarrassment and hatred for James, for his growing, brutal contempt of me. And that's where we kept clutching at each other with the ferocity of knowing how horribly wrong we were to fuck each other.

And that's where I will bring you, my child, years from now. You will be innocent. I will be sad. I might tell you that you were here before. You won't believe me.

I wouldn't want to believe it either, standing in this barren triangle of sand and rain.

Fifth day of November

Often I see the same shape on top of the hill behind the village, like a tall tree, or a man, or perhaps a cross, standing stark against the soft cold mist, with the sun at its early afternoon angle seeming to single it out from everything else with an outline of very pale gold. Today I went to sketch it, but it's difficult to capture. I only have color, light, shadow. While the air has depth and substance and distance. I think of it as a mountain crowned with light.

The chill of the air got in the way of my patience. Also the permanent chill of the fear I have inside me. And who could possibly paint with cold feet?

I was disappointed, though, and sad.

I went for a walk then, down along the shore. There, too, everything was colorful, but alien to me and separate. It's a world complete in itself, nothing to do with me and useless to me in its mute splendor. It doesn't have the power to touch me as strongly as I want it to. Back to the road again, along the ditch where even now the red small fuchsia blossoms hold their own against the season. How tiny the blossoms are for shining with such violence in their bright harmlessness. Suddenly the sun came out, undiluted by clouds.

I reached the first buildings, empty brown earth of fields between them. Empty, yes, but not yet deserted. There was a haystack, never brought in, useless now after too much rain. On top of it a large white cat sunned itself. Muscles tense as though expanding themselves as far as they would stretch to bask in the last possibility of sun. I ached at seeing this. My whole being felt flooded with goodbyes.

In my sitting room three letters waited for me. Reassurances that the network of friends was still intact. But for how long? How much of it will remain undamaged?

Sixth day of November

It's way past midnight now. My mind still spinning from incense and Latin phrases.

We had mass at the house tonight for the old folks in the village who can't make it to church on Sundays. I went out of politeness, curiosity, and hunger for atonement.

I didn't even get a chance to kneel properly. Sat on my stool, crammed in between the edge of the sofa, the back of a heavy man, the shoulder of a standing child. So I slid against the corner of the chair in front of me, my knees suspended, bent halfway between floor and chair, my elbow supporting my weight on the brown armrest of the sofa. I watched the priest. The soft folds of his robe flowed gently with every movement he made. I admire the ritual, although it doesn't belong to me and can't comfort me. I admired most of all the strong swift motion of his arm, softened by wide sleeves, with which he thrusts the golden chalice up toward God.

The men and women knelt in whatever fashion they could. Must have been hard for some of the old ones, even where there was plenty of room. They knelt on the floor, fenced in by other awkward limbs, wrapped in thick shapeless coats, the sweetness of faith carved into the wrinkles of their faces, and tiredness and sickness carved into their worn, hunched bodies.

They do not carry children in their bodies.

Those of them who did are long absolved from shame or gossip or rejection.

Or so it seems. Gossip and rejection may well be eternal. The woman found drunk on the road three times last month was there. And the woman who lives alone in the stone house by the edge of the water, regardless of floods and storms, ever since her wayward husband left her there.

How do I fit in? The only thing that distinguishes me is that my shame and my sin aren't known yet, not yet a matter for public discussion.

After blessing the holy water, and then half an hour of piously restrained chatter, the priest said goodnight and left.

As though on cue, Mrs. O'Neil and her sister whipped the lace off the table, replaced it with red and white plastic and served at long last the chicken that had been cooking in the kitchen all along, its aroma masked by holy incense. Everyone fell to, like a congregation of sly foxes, chewing with conspiratorial grins. Including myself, once I was able to stop laughing.

It seems that if I try to kneel with them and can't, but try anyway and suddenly succeed somehow, it is to them that I kneel, not to some unwieldy, alien God, but to the society of those who blunder, sin, and still belong.

I'm more certain every day. And there's nothing more precious to me right now.

I know I will be alone in this. Not even that frightens me at the moment.

The neighbors' six-year-old girl kissed my hand today. The lightest touch, like a flower petal falling on my hand. I was so surprised. I never knew she liked me so much. Or is it you, child, whom she senses and greets with her innocence that's not yet tainted by proprieties? Tomorrow she'll have forgotten her kiss, but I will not forget. After you are born, they will keep her away from me with enigmatic silence that will disturb and hurt her. Until she forgets that silence too.

I'll have to move to a city so that I can find some job to support us. There will be little help from others. We won't need it. Who, after all, could I turn to? My parents? After some time perhaps. By then I may be too proud. My sister? Not while she's attached to her reputable husband. Friends? They might offer sympathy, romantic encouragement, or lofty advice. One can't subsist on those. One subsists on money and food and shelter.

The dream is to find someone who has both money and romantic notions and who needs a cause. A fallen woman, for example, who would rise again to the savior's credit.

What drivel I write. It's important for me to determine, quickly, whom I can trust. Everyone whose heart might be on my side is, it seems, also meshed in deeper loyalties. And who are we, my unborn one and I, to tear through all their complicated artifice of living in the manner they understand best?

What I need is an artifice of living of my own.

I'll have to move to the city and find work. Soon.

Eighth day of November

I must have an abortion. I can't have one in this country. So, obviously, it's time to make travel arrangements.

I can't sit here and wait and let things take care of themselves. They won't.

Suddenly I see my last lover stand on the lawn in his garden, a few days before I left to come here, asking as though in defiance of my leaving: "And what are you going to do about birth control?" My wanting to shout at him, "None of your damn business." My saying instead, "I won't need it." "Well, you had better be careful then," he said, "because you won't be able to get an abortion where you are going."

How I hated then. Not him. Not myself. Not even the occasion. But the brutality of existence that makes everything a matter of consequence and calculation. You can do anything in heaven or on earth so long as it doesn't show. A filling womb and a baby show. Oh, awkwardly.

And so I will quietly and calculatingly go on a journey, go through the appropriate humiliation of finding the right people, then reemerge as the untouched, untouchable child-woman again. With this difference, that I will forever have this secret on my mind.

It must be done. No matter what the secret will cost me. Someone, give me the strength now to make plans. Because the truth is that I cannot have a child. My body may be able to bear one, but my heart's essence is still child itself, drifting, without responsibility or purpose, glittering without the burden of reality.

Ninth day of November

It's rained for so many days now. I feel trapped inside this house, these two tiny rooms. Ought to ask someone for a lift into town to get supplies and start working again. I keep making excuses. One day I get up too late to make it worth my while, the next day it's too cold to go, the third day it's something else.

I keep wanting to hide and avoid. Once a day I walk to the post office, out of a sense of duty to myself and to those who always seem to be watching me, so that they can see me walk about and don't have cause to ask if anything is wrong with me. If only I had someone to confide in, someone to take care of me, to make decisions I don't seem to be able to make and don't want to make.

Today I made myself ill with the impulse to call James, and with the counter poison reason that made me, finally, resist the temptation. The public phone booth across the street from the post office was like a turning magnet, attracting, repelling. What a world where phone numbers still have precisely one digit.

I yearned to talk to James, to unload some of my burden. And who else would be more appropriate? But then I pictured him standing in his little shop, customers listening to his side of the conversation, James himself floored by the news, no doubt wanting to deny, wanting to convince himself this must be some mistake. A ruse. A strategy to ensnare him. I couldn't bear that. And so I had to, in the end, remain alone.

And God only knows, the telephone operator would probably listen in on the call. I wouldn't put it past her to be riveted by my dilemma. Our dilemma.

Poor James. The only reason I would rouse him out of his male complacency would be if there were a chance that I might die. Sometimes death seems amazingly desirable now. It would be the easiest solution by far.

But what will happen to you, child, if I die? Who will be with you then? I would not live with you in tiny rooms in cities, loving you and waiting for your love to grow for me. I wouldn't be there to hear your first small cries, your later, larger disillusions. I couldn't protect you, touch you, shelter you.

But also I wouldn't be there to hinder you. For if I died, they would accept you far more easily. If only I could manage to die at the right time, I wouldn't stand in your way of being protected by those whose protection would probably be far more powerful than mine. It would be easier for you. Pity for some little, helpless being, never mind its mother's sins, would then be in their hearts to cradle you. Poor bastard, poor little innocent waif.

We'd have to be so terribly brave if I lived. But if I died, you could grow, lovely like a tree, in the sun and water of their protection. And for me, the burden of your coming would be resolved.

I would rather that you tore me into death with your coming than that I should ever hinder you or harm you. As I have already done.

Forgive me, little one, my unborn one. I was so lonely. I didn't know there was this possibility of giving you the life that I myself have often seemed so utterly incapable of living well, even though I grew to love it beyond belief.

If you are lucky, you will be a boy. Your brothers would more easily accept you. If you're a girl, I hope that you will

not be born to be sacrificed. I am so tired. I hope that your
life will be warm.

Tenth day of November

Puzzled by a dream last night.

I dreamt about children. A girl and a boy, both blond,
big-eyed, very young. They took me by the hands, one at each
side, and led me to their mother's house. I'd received a letter
from her in which she asked me to become her lover. I felt
apprehensive, for I knew, even within the haze of my dream,
that I didn't know how to make love to a woman. But I also
felt warmth and tenderness inside, knowing, almost without
effort, that I would never refuse a woman who asked for my
love. In all the mist of dream and puzzlement, I recognized
clearly that I could refuse a man's love easily, but if a woman
were to call me, I would not hesitate to go to her.

We found the children's mother waiting for us on a
wide deep bed, framed in heavy polished wood. I lay down
beside her on a blanket that was silky and fragrant, like fresh
summer grass. I put my cheek against her cheek, my hand
against her hand. That seemed to be enough. The children
were lying between us. But, though I was part of the shelter
for them, I too felt sheltered, and fresh, as though I had been
washed clean of all fears.

I don't know what this dream means. But I felt
comforted all day.

Eleventh day of November

I could love you, Jamie! I will not call you James again.

Yes, I could even marry him. We would build our love on a cornerstone of kindness. I would be forever faithful to him if he married me. How could I not be faithful to the father of my lovely growing child?

I would help you with everything, Jamie. I would bring you flowers, rings, and all beautiful things. If you would teach me the reality of loving, then I would teach you everything beautiful on earth. We would not be alone.

I have no right to love Jamie, but I love him already.

Jamie, I seem to have so much in this world. But I still need your comfort, your protection. I will create things. And whatever I have I will bring to you. If you will bring me protection for my child, then I will bring you sunlight and flowers and things far better even than life. Let me be yours.

I have watched women care for their men. I could easily do what they do. I could sweep the doorstep of my husband's house with pride.

Look, I will bring you a drink of water to the shop, or out into the fields when you are working, Jamie. Later I will greet you with a cup of love as you come home. I will ask for very little. Only this, that once, when I am old, you will be kind enough to touch my hair with tenderness and with forgiveness. I will be good to you. I will deserve your gratitude and, possibly, your love.

Goodbye, the rest of you. Farewell to everything that is not mine.

I will come to your house like a beggar, Jamie, with nothing to bring but our child. But I will win your mother and your father over to my side. I will build a rainbow bridge between their first mistrust and the reality of our child. I can't always be running. Settle me in a small house by the sea.

I will draw in the wings that I have spread into the world, as sails are drawn when they have carried everything safely into the harbor, and I will fold them softly around the child, around that one strong center. And when you see us so, Jamie, you too will be touched with pity for the child. I'll show you the way, the enfolding motion. Only, please let us live, give us protection. Let us live!

Twelfth day of November

No, I don't need protection. I will take care of us.

I'll move to the city with you, my pride. Or, rather, with you and with my pride. We'll live in a gray house, dank with anonymity. I'll find some woman too poor to judge us, my child. Yes, someone with too much poverty to refuse to tend you while I am gone during the day. I don't even care if she has warts on her cheeks and mats in her hair. Or foul and common thoughts in her head.

I'll rise early each morning when the streets are still sluggish with dawn, and I'll find work in a factory, turning wheels, or gathering and sorting other people's fragments, doing their chores. But in the evenings, my little one, I will be home to claim you. We'll have a small cramped room somewhere. But it will be full of light. I'll find a long blue skirt to wear, a blue woolen skirt, to add warmth to the thin light of some cheap lamp. I will hold you and cradle you in the warmth of my dreams, spinning around you first touch, later songs, later words. We won't need anyone else.

One day I will bring you here. No one will remember me. We'll pass through this village. We'll walk out to the ocean. Then we'll walk down the road to the barren place where you were conceived. We'll stand there, hand in hand.

I'll tell you all that happened there. You won't want to believe me. If we are lucky, you will laugh. And I'll laugh with you, laugh at how easily all my proud, ambitious, precious past will have fallen away from me, from us. The rain that wiped out tracks of tires will have wiped out, over the years, all my bitterness as well.

No, you won't believe me. Perhaps, to make you laugh again, I'll talk of some mysterious highborn stranger whom I chanced to meet and lie with in a golden flash of destiny.

Perhaps then you might want to believe me. Perhaps then I could find atonement for the loud and grimy roads I will have dragged you through for years of hopelessness and loneliness and work, and ugly women who would tend you for a few pennies a day.

Thirteenth day of November

I am so alone.

I am so afraid.

I pray that my child won't be ugly or deformed.

Mrs. O'Neil came in this morning with an apple and a slice of fresh bread, still warm. I took her gifts. I might as well get used to a lifetime of gifts and having to accept. I saw the usual animation in her face, flickers of triumph that, yes, they bought three rolls of wire fence today, cheaply, a true bargain, to put around the yard in the spring. Flickers of contempt. The old maid from down the street who drinks too much stopped at the house today to use the telephone. Flickers of love and pride. How her homely thirteen-year-old son won a spelling prize in school today.

How I wish I could be part of all this mix of innocence and strong convictions, of unfiltered, undiluted life.

After she left again, I drank a glass of water. She told me once I shouldn't drink it from the tap. But what do I care? I looked in the mirror over the sink. My face looked bloated. The eyes wide and red, and veins of fear running through them.

There's still an almost full bottle of tonic wine under my bed. Sticky sweetness that would lull me out of time into forgetfulness. Just for a while. Just now.

If only I had someone already born to talk to.

Oh, child of a woman with red eyes and a stomach ill with fear like vermin crawling, forgive me that I have to make your coming so difficult and filled with apprehension.

It will pass. It will pass.

I love you already. And that peacefulness in me is you.

Fourteenth day of November

I walked to town today and bought school notebooks. It was the best I could find. If I remove the staples in the center, the blank pages will do for sketching.

Must get a ride to the city next week. Maybe with Mrs. O'Neil's sister-in-law. Made five calls and actually found a place that seems to carry some of the supplies I want. I can't just leave here one fine future day with no new work to show.

I have action fever, hardly time to write.

It snowed today, early in the morning. The sky is a mélange of everything from pink to black.

End of dreaming: Blessed blood between my thighs.

SARAH

I don't know where to begin.

This here is Zack, by the way. I call him Zack. His dad didn't like it at first, but later he called him Zack, too. I didn't want to call him by some highfaluting name that everybody is bound to make fun of, or stumbles over, you know.

Anyway, doesn't Zack have the most gorgeous hazel eyes? I'm not big on God these days, but sometimes I think God, or somebody, poured light into Zack's eyes, so that it must now always radiate out.

Sorry, Zack. I know I promised I wouldn't talk about you like you weren't even in the room or something. Of course you are here. Come, sit right here on my lap. Then, if I do talk about you, maybe it won't feel so strange. That's right, put your head just here. Are you comfy?

We never want to be apart again, if we can help it. If I can help it anyways. Isn't that right, Zack? At least not until Zack is much older. And even then I'll always make sure you know where I am, Zack. You'll always know. I promise. As long as I . . . forever.

You want to know how I met my husband?

I was working as a waitress at Rubio's of the Rockies. He came in with a bunch of guys one night. It was four of them together that time. I hadn't seen any of them before. But it's a tourist town, so that's pretty normal. They ate their steaks and drank their beers, and I tried to do my best to earn a good tip. They were watching TV in the corner. Have you been to Rubio's? The TV hangs down at an angle from over the left side of the bar. It's not very big. But the volume you get out of it is plenty loud. Plenty. Even with all the tables filled and everybody yakking about one thing or another, until it just becomes a sort of rumble of noise and smoke. Yeah, we still let folks smoke at Rubio's. I smoke myself. I didn't while I was pregnant with Zack, and I'm proud of that. But afterwards I started again.

Abe never even seemed to notice me at first. But then he asked my name. They'd paid their bill already, and they were making a ruckus, talking about this and that, discussing the equipment of some cheerleaders on the TV screen, and I was hanging around because it looked like he was fishing in his pocket. For a tip, I hoped. I was being extra pleasant because you can always use a tip. I wasn't exactly swimming in dough, though I've always managed. He looked like he might leave a good tip, too, if only to impress his buddies. I can tell the type. So I hung around trying to ingratiate myself without being too obvious about it.

"Let's ask this lady here," he said at some point, patting me on the rump. You got to let them do that. I learned that early on. It doesn't mean anything. "What's your name?" he asked.

"Sarah," I said.

He stopped speaking and looked at me for the first time full on. It was a deep, strange, fascinated look. It was a surprised look, rather flattering. I didn't know then that any Sarah would have done.

Nobody said a word for a while. The rumble continued at the other tables, but at this table time stood still, chilled.

"Will you marry me, Sarah?" he finally asked.

"Well, it's a bit sudden and all that." In those days I still gave good for good. But that's all water under the bridge now. "And I don't even know your name yet."

"You're my witnesses," he said to his buddies. "I will marry this woman."

His buddies changed over the years. But they're always the same type. Nobody hangs with him too long.

Zack, you're heavy when you wiggle so much. Are you bored? Do you want to go over there and play with those nice Duplo for a while? Build a new bridge? Or a stadium? Go on. We'll be right here talking. Go on.

I thought it just was a particularly tasteless way of flirting with me. Like this guy I met in college once. This was a poet, and until then I had always kind of admired poets. I wrote some poetry myself, but it wasn't anything to ever show to anybody else. It was just for myself. This guy was published, though. He was about twice my age and his breath smelled of cheap red wine. Somebody introduced us, and he said, "Oh, my next wife?" It made me angry. I kind of knew he said that to everybody he met, and wife to him meant someone in the sack, and I was so young then, that kind of talk still bothered me a lot.

Yeah, I went to junior college for a while, but it bored me. Not that being a waitress is a major thrill. Still it feels better somehow. I feel I'm more my own person, instead of trying to figure out what everybody wants me to say or think at any given time, so that I can then get some diploma. For what exactly? To make more money, so I can get a larger apartment, and a fancier car? I just don't function that way. The only time I regret not having a lot of money is this situation right now. I'll get to that in a minute.

Anyway, back then at Rubio's I went along with his joking for a bit. But it wasn't a joke to him.

He actually meant it.

I still work there at Rubio's, yes. I mean, I did until two weeks ago. And I just know they'll take me back when all this is sorted out. They're always short people.

You see, I never thought of marrying anymore. I was forty-six when I met Abe, and I liked my life well enough the way it was. I liked being independent, not having to answer to anyone.

But he didn't take no for an answer. He said we'd, well, have a fine boy. That's what he said. I laughed. At my age? I should have a grandchild. I wanted to use birth control. I even told him to go look for somebody younger, and then he could have a whole station wagon size family, or minivan or whatever they call it nowadays.

To which he said, "But I've never met anyone named Sarah before."

Which struck me as, like, where has he been? I think Sarahs are a dime a dozen. There were three of us when I went to first grade. I remember because I was kind of upset that there were so many of us all at once and I wasn't anything special anymore. Somebody called our name, and three of us weren't sure, was it us, or one of the others?

Abe telling me he wouldn't find himself another woman because he'd never met anybody called Sarah before, that wasn't when we first met. We'd already dated for a while, or whatever you call it. Not real dates, you know, with dinner and movies, and so on. I hardly wanted to go to a restaurant for a date and pay to have someone else wait on me when I could eat at Rubio's for free. I wasn't interested in dating all that much anyway. Like I said, I like to be my own woman. But he had his mind set on me. You know how men can be when they want something.

There's this weird stuff about men—how we can be strong on our own as women, but as soon as we get on the radar of a guy, all the strength just sort of gets sucked out. I was doing fine, and suddenly here comes this guy into my life.

We were married when I was just short of forty-seven, and we had Zack ten months later.

He's hard to deny, my husband.

But one time I did. I was already pregnant with Zack. I got pregnant pretty much right away after we married and Abe insisted I stop using birth control. For a while he wanted me to not tell any of his buddies that I was his wife. And then he wanted me to put out for them. He said the Eskimos did that for their guests, and it was a friendly gesture. That time I got out of it, though. I'm not an Eskimo, thank you very much.

"Abe," I said to him, "I don't know what all your fantasies are, and I'm your wife, and I'll do all kinds of stuff for you. But that? No."

Amazingly, he let it go at that without any more argument. Thank God. I don't know what I would have done if he had gone on and insisted.

But then Zack was born, and things were good. I never thought I'd love having a child so much. I guess with me being so old already, it felt extra special. Maybe I was calmer, too, and didn't have so many ambitions for myself as I might have had as a younger woman. You know, where it might have gotten on my nerves that I didn't have a full minute to myself anymore in a day. I really love the boy.

My husband spent most of his free time with his buddies.

"Abe-raw-ham." I wonder if anybody ever called him that.

His buddies kept on changing. Monthly? Weekly? It was hard to keep track of. He'd bring them home to watch a game, and they always looked sort of the same. Tough guys, you know, the outdoorsy variety, woodsy smells, knives somewhere on their person, even if it was only a pocket knife. But no matter who they were at any given time, he was always sort of the leader of the pack. I think he insisted on that, wouldn't have it any other way. Kind of attractive to have a leader around. As a woman you think you'll be taken care of. And the men seemed to like to have someone with his kind of authority around, someone who told them what to do and they didn't have to think for themselves so much. Sort of like in the military. Guys like that, you know. So Abe's buddies seemed to like his authority, at least for a while. Until he hurt them, their pride, something like that. It wouldn't surprise me if he hurt them deliberately, but always in ways they could never prove. Then they drifted away. But there was always a new guy to take their place.

The day they went up into the mountains, I made them roast beef sandwiches and packed a big slice of pound cake for all of them. And beef jerky, and egg stuff you can just mix up with water, and trail mix. I thought Zack was a bit young for going on this so-called hiking trip. But Abe said he was going to make a man out of the boy, and the earlier the better. Obviously, between him and his buddies, they were going to be able to protect the little one from anything dangerous.

Zack was excited about the outing, believe you me. I mean, they were taking him seriously. They were taking him on a hiking trip as though he were one of them. A dream come true for the little tyke. He almost couldn't fall asleep the night before. But when he finally did, he went out like a light. In parts of myself I was proud and excited for Zack, too. Now he was going to get his first lessons in how to be a man among men.

By then I already knew, of course, that Abe had this fixation on the Abraham and Sarah and Isaac story from the Bible, but, well, obviously we weren't them. She had her Isaac when she was ninety. Besides, that Abraham was in a different league from my guy with his Rockports and his parka and mountain gear. And our Zack was just a regular blond American kid.

Anyway, on that trip Abe did manage to lose his buddies for a while, and, yes, he did tie Zack to a rock. Zack freaked and Abe had his fun. There was no ram, no nothing. Just fear and vicious power. But Abe got the boy back home in one piece. That's the main thing in the end.

God, while this went on, I was at home imagining them striding along with the wind caressing their skin, and birds swooping around them, crows and starlings and such, and song birds twittering from their perches. I imagined Zack playing with the yellow butterflies, hoping to catch them, wanting his father to catch them for him no doubt, and disappointed that his father wouldn't. Or couldn't, perhaps.

A situation like that is easily disguised by an adult claiming he wouldn't.

"How was it?" I asked when they came back.

"It was fine."

Zack acted weird, though. He was surly and quiet. He'd always been a sunny kid before. Now he mumbled and didn't look me in the eyes. I thought something had scared him. Could have been anything.

It's easier to see a certain dignity about all this the way it's described in the Bible. The boy asking, "Father, where's the lamb for the sacrifice?"

In reality, there's nothing dignified about it whatsoever. Here's merely a big guy terrorizing a little one, just because he can. That's all there is to it, no matter how many voices of God he claims to have heard, no matter how he rationalizes that it's all part of growing up to be a man. It's vicious bully stuff, nothing more and nothing less. Abe weighs two hundred and sixty-eight pounds on a light day. Zack weighs thirty-seven. Can you imagine?

You see, Zack trusted his father. What else would he do? His father, up till then, was everything to him.

Zack probably screamed. No, Dad. Don't hurt me. Mom. Help. Dad. No. Dad!

Zack didn't want to talk about it at all. Makes sense to me. Abe probably even warned him not to say a word. But Zack moaned about his father in his nightmares, and that's how I started getting the truth out of him. I went nuts. I packed up a suitcase and got us on a train to California. It's been a whirlwind ever since.

Why California? Warm weather, I guess. I didn't know how we were going to live exactly, and I didn't want us to be cold. I wanted to get into a shelter like this one, although I didn't quite know how you did that yet. I just wanted to get lost with Zack so that Abe wouldn't find us.

Abe always sounds so reasonable in person, you know.

So did the cops when they caught up with us in California. They sounded so reassuring. And Zack wasn't all that happy on the road either. The cops kept saying everything was going to be all right. Did he hurt you? they asked. Zack truthfully said, no, his dad had just tied him up. But he had said he would cut him. For God.

Abe had already told the police his Abraham story, and how it was all just a dramatization. And they believed him. Because, I guess he always did talk so believably, like I said.

Meanwhile, in my heart, it's all killer stuff. God. Etc. I mean, Son of Sam heard God's voice, didn't he? At least they finally put him away. And the original Abraham—well, in my opinion, they should have put him away, too, rather than glorify him for all posterity for doing what he did. I mean what else did he ever do that was all that remarkable? His claim to fame was his unwavering belief in God, even when God told him to sacrifice his son. But then again, look at their religion. I'm not much for church myself. Their God himself sets up his own son for slaughter. They admire that as God's sacrifice for human redemption. Sounds like a rationalization to me. So what do you expect from a God like that? I think it's just our job to be human on earth, never mind gods and their demands, and church fathers and how they would like to train us to be something other than human instead.

Anyway, I'm scared now. But I have to be brave. I know that. I don't know what exactly they'll do. Abe isn't allowed near us while we're here in the shelter—and we have a restraining order, too, just in case. But when I last saw him, he gave me a magazine to read, with an article earmarked. A message for me. About how they are jailing women nowadays for not protecting their children from abuse when they should have known, should have done something.

I'm afraid. I would have been scared without that article, too. I haven't done anything wrong, you know. But that doesn't necessarily count. Not under the law, which promises justice, but it's a justice that can be bought, it appears.

I don't want to be separated from Zack. He needs me now, more than ever. You've seen me talk to him as though I'm confident. Inside me, there's no such thing as confidence. I feel like jelly. And if they take him away from me, he'll know that I haven't been able to keep my promise. And if that ever happens, then will he ever be able to trust anything again? I wonder whether he will hate me one day anyhow for not being able to protect him from this weird stuff to begin with.

You know, I used to think I wasn't all that dumb, what with school and my good grades and all that, but it seems I've been really dumb to have landed myself in a situation like this.

Trouble is, men with their laws and their God and their self-confidence can always speak so much reason and charm, and then, once they've got you in a snare, it seems so hard to get out again. I feel all clumsy.

I wish someone would come and tell me what to do. Or at least approve of what I do. It used to be all I had to do was make nice. I've always wanted to please. But this new place in my life asks for stronger stuff. I don't know what exactly I need to say or do to keep us safe.

I love this child. I want to protect him. Listen to that laughter, even when he plays by himself. Isn't he beautiful?

I don't know where this will end.

THE DOLL ELIZABETH

This morning he made love to me. His face was like a wolf's face. I love that, his teeth bared like a snarl. For me it was okay. It doesn't matter that I don't enjoy it as much as he does. Now it is night again, after the show, and I wish I could put my hands around his neck and watch him sleep, but I don't want to touch him. It might wake him up. He needs his sleep.

I don't really know this man.

I have heard other girls whisper loud enough for me to hear. How lucky I am to have him. How they can't understand what he sees in me. It worries me a little. What if it's true? What if one day he wakes up and thinks it was a mistake to marry me?

Mom warned me about that because I am only eighteen and he is already twenty-nine. I told her she was just jealous because I got what I wanted. It wasn't a nice thing to say.

I never told her how I prayed for him.

I love the way he touches me. Same fingers that strum and caress his guitar and made him famous. When I saw him in concert for the first time I snuck backstage because his long dark hair was so beautiful. I stuttered something. He smiled.

I listen to his sleep breath, but I cannot sleep.

He told me once about going on stage with a band and getting the audience all worked up, which then loops energy back to the band. There's no more delicious experience than that, he said. Not even sex.

I think of the doll I once wanted, with sleep eyes and long blond braided hair. I got her for Christmas. She was almost as tall as I was. Her eyes did open and close. I called her Elizabeth after my older brother's beautiful girlfriend. I undid her braids and thought I could fix her hair some other way, let it hang loose down her back for example. It didn't work. The hair fell back into the shape it originally had, although not braided now. Six long synthetic pieces hanging down in twisted strands. So I braided them again. That did work, though it was a bit boring to know she'd always have these braids.

I had wished for her ardently. The sleep eyes, the long hair. And here she was. Somewhere there is a photo of me with the doll. I'm grinning from ear to ear. She's her usual serene self. Beyond that first attempt at undoing and redoing her hair, I didn't really know what to do with her. I could make her sit and stand and lie on her back, at which point she closed her eyes. Soon I put her in a toy carriage I already owned, together with my smaller dolls and some stuffed animals, including a bald teddy bear whom I had successfully given a haircut several years before. Once they were all in the carriage, I would read travel ads and imagine we were going on a journey somewhere.

I remember mostly the loveliness of yearning for her, hoping, praying—but silently and privately—because I knew it would be considered wrong to pray for a toy when there were hungry children in the world. Those were the days when waiting for Christmas was better than Christmas itself. And then the moment of unwrapping her and holding her in my arms.

Same as with Tommy, really. How I yearned for him. His lovely long dark hair. So I went backstage to meet him. I did it again. I prayed. Secretly.

Marriage has always looked interesting on other people. Two lovers walking off hand in hand into some misty fairy tale future. This is no fairy tale of course. Sure Tommy looks like a prince onstage, but in reality there are all these cables to the mic and to his green and silver electric guitar. Who ever heard of cables in a fairy tale?

I am filled with yearning again, yearning for myself this time. What will I do now? I can't put him in a toy carriage and look at travel brochures. Sometimes I yearn for the hunger. I have all I have ever wanted. What will I do with it?

WOODCUT

She was seventeen. Her heart was scanning the world when it unexpectedly fell open. He stood in the hallway of her weekend host's house, with a fold-up easel under his left arm. His skin was the color of chestnuts. Her hair was the color of wheat.

"Abe," he introduced himself. "Some friends call me Ape, though."

She had to go to some stupid Snow Ball Dance with a blind date. It was on the schedule for the weekend while Abe was not.

"I'll wait up for you at Kathy's house," he said. And he did. They sat on a single soft chair in the living room until 1:30 a.m. Then he had to go home. He touched her lips one more time. "See you in morning."

Morning came. He gave her a tour of the old school he had attended. He was twenty-one now, away in college on a scholarship.

On Sunday after church she went to have dinner with his family, a younger sister, cautious, and two younger brothers who clung to her. The parents were kind, pretending no one noticed her white skin.

He took her to the bus station on Sunday afternoon. He carried her bags. "What's in there?" he asked. "Bricks?"

She blushed. "Books." She hadn't opened one since Friday.

"Well, you can read them on the bus," he said. She knew she wouldn't.

"I'll see you again," she promised when he gave her the last of his magical kisses.

"Sure," he said. She didn't believe it any more than he did.

She sat in the far back of the bus and waved until he was out of sight and even a little longer afterward. Then she collapsed in her seat and sobbed. She knew her life had changed and she felt homeless.

"Are you okay?" a woman asked.

"Yes." Her jaw was trembling. She wanted to be left alone with the immensity of it all, and, luckily, they let her be.

She didn't want to go back home at all. The grass would be gray now, she thought, and so it was for a good long while. School was dull. Old ambitions tasted like cardboard.

Life went on.

He went to Nairobi to teach English for two years. She wanted to go, but it wasn't allowed. She sent him fourteen letters, wanting to send more. He sent her nine. One included a woodcut, black ink on cream-colored paper with a tear drop on the face of a girl who resembled her. "See, I've made your face black, too," he wrote.

She married him on her twentieth birthday. At first she had wanted to wait till she was twenty-one, but in the end she wasn't that patient.

People warned them it would be difficult. It was. If anyone can do it, we can, she thought obstinately. They parted twelve years later on good terms. He was overbearing in an attractive way. She was unable to withstand the power of his masculine self-confidence. She loved him still and trusted he felt the same about her.

He remarried a few years later, one of his own kind, a beautiful woman named Leesha whom he had dated back in high school. It was right. Nevertheless it hurt.

He contracted a debilitating disease in his early forties. For a while they exchanged emails in the early mornings. But then Leesha went on his computer and read one of their recent exchanges and accused him of being in love with his first blond wife still, and she in turn quietly withdrew for all their sakes.

She visited the couple once. Leesha was kind. When Leesha left the living room for a phone call, Abe reached out and touched his former wife's arm with a trembling hand. "You're exquisite," he said.

"Thank you. As are you," she replied.

She did not visit again. He was ravaged with drugs, for blood thinning, for depression, for all manner of things. She remembered his brilliant, incisive mind.

She didn't know if Leesha would let her know when he died. It didn't matter. She had said her goodbyes so long ago. She was grateful for the complicated years together and that one weekend of kisses when she was seventeen.

The woodcut was on sturdy paper and kept well through the years.

I KNOW

Today they took my clothes away. Oh, I know what they want.

I think I still have a right to try and see Brendan sit with me here in this mist, though he is gone now.

I have a right to reject strangers. The woman who says her name is Monica. Perhaps so. But my real Monica is a little girl who brings me a trout she has caught to cook at the cabin.

I have a right to spend time with Brian on a cold mountain in Mexico, like the one from the postcard he sent. I want to warn him, that woman with him, she plans to destroy something. I don't trust her. Already half of his jacket is lopped off.

I have a right to the laughter of my friends, there, in the cathedral, giggling in the vestibule over my fishnet stockings under the prim white organdy, with Brendan already waiting at the altar.

I always liked fairy tales. Who doesn't? When you are obedient and good, you get rewarded.

It smells strange here.

I have always been obedient. Well, almost always. My skin hurts. Don't push me like that. I don't want that. Gentle. Please.

Maybe this is my reward for obedience. This fog of gentleness. There, a piece of clear sky through the scraps of fog. Brendan again. But I better protect him with mist again. There. A thick veil. They left me flannel nightgowns and underwear. Soft. It is all I need, they said.

They are so wrong. I still need you, Brendan. You wouldn't have let this happen. And the children. I need them. Not these impatient imposters. Anyone can use any old name.

I know what they are doing.

I love the mist in these mountains.

HER FAIRY TALE

I always thought she killed my mother. No, she didn't wield a gun or a knife or even poison. She just added anguish after anguish until my fragile mother broke. I stood by helpless. Maybe in my helplessness I was the killer after all. An accomplice in any event.

First she put Mother in a home. Mother fought it till the bitter end. She loved living alone, had done so since Dad died way back when. But Julie wanted the house. It's for the children, she always said. Your mother is a single woman. We have three children. Your mother is rich. We live in near squalor in a shabby apartment.

Mother didn't want to go to a home. People lose their spirit there, she told me. You know that, Tony, she said. Don't let her make me go. Everyone I've ever known who went inside was dead within two years. I don't want to go. I am okay by myself. Your father bought me this house. I am not leaving.

Maybe it's best, I told her.

It's expensive, she said. I'd be able to live much more frugally here. Besides, your Julie just wants the place for herself. Mark my words, for herself. Not for the children as she always says. Not for the family. Not for you.

How can you say that, Mother?

How can I not, Tony? When I'm in the home, you'll move in here, right? So why not let me stay? The place is big enough. She'll never have to see me.

Mother tried hard, but she didn't prevail. Mother kept citing the expense, and over and over she said she'd rather die than go into a home. Besides, it was a death sentence anyway.

In early August, Mother slipped in the bathtub. In the fall, in time for school, she was in a home and we moved into the house.

The home was a nice one, down by the lake, with the luxury of a single room apartment for her, when many of the other old folks had to share a room. Her two windows overlooked the lake. She often sat by one window or the other watching birds.

We moved into the house I had grown up in, Julie, the kids, and I.

It's for the kids, Julie said. This will be great for the kids.

Mark my words, Mother said as she sat by a window, looking out at birds, not meeting my eyes, her hands twisting the soft gray blanket in her lap. I'll be gone in two years.

Julie didn't have that much patience. She visited Mother often and always left her agitated about the enormous expense.

You wanted me to be here, Mother would shout at Julie.

But you could make an effort to stay well, Julie shouted back. Every time you sneeze it costs hundreds of dollars extra. And take your blood pressure medication, for God's sake. You're not the doctor, you can't just declare you don't need it. And then Julie would itemize to Mother the dollars she was costing. It was painful for Mother. She had always been frugal despite being a wealthy widow.

Mark my words, Mother said to me, she'll needle me to death, and then she'll leave you and take half of your inheritance with her, or more. It's for the kids, she will say.

Julie wouldn't leave me. I was sure of that. Julie and I had been together for nearly twenty-five years if you counted the years we lived together before we were married when our oldest was conceived and born, Keith. Then we had Emily, and finally Mark.

She'll leave you, and she'll take everything she can get, mark my words, Mother said.

No way would she leave me. No way.

She'll say it's for the children.

When Mother died from a weak heart and a prescribed increase in medication she didn't want to take in the first place and that her already fragile condition couldn't handle, I felt lost for a while. I knew I should have done more to protect her. Now she was gone, really gone. The woman who had given me life was gone. I had wanted to spend more years exchanging observations, and even memories of Dad who had died so early that Julie never knew him.

Julie grieved, too, in her own way, and more than I expected her to. Her Facebook posts were filled with tributes to Mother who in retrospect was the best and most unforgettable mother figure in all the world.

I was lost for many months. When I finally began finding myself again, I noticed things had changed. Julie and I fought constantly. She found fault with me all the time. There was hardly any affection left, few kind words. She was always angry with me. Sex never came into the picture at all anymore. I remember our last time, a few weeks before Mother died. I felt like I was not giving her enough pleasure, and I suspect she felt so too.

You're the love of my life, Julie once told me. I'm so glad you are in my life and on my side.

That had changed now, it would appear. Now there was only strife and anger and disappointment.

What can I do to make things well for us again, I asked her one day.

She was in mid-rant about one of my many shortcomings. I wish you'd just die, she said.

I'm not going to die, I said, so you'll just have to prepare to pack your bags and leave.

Or you will, she said.

I laughed. You'd kick me out of the house I was born and raised in? I sneered. For the children?

Her eyes widened when I preempted her customary justification by saying it before she got around to it.

Julie is beautiful. A little heavy around her middle lately, but her auburn hair still turns heads, and she is more slender than a whole bunch of teenage girls you see these days.

I'm not quite so attractive. A bit fleshy, all that good food, and she loved going out to eat, and so on. Until I got sick, of course, but even skinny, I'm no prize.

I keep remembering how I first fell in love with her. The endless kisses by the lake under the willow, me kissing her and swatting off bugs. How she called me her prince when I gave her a present. She was a receptionist at a clinic. I was the wealthy widow's son who could afford flowers, excellent champagne, fine chocolates, a diamond or two now and again.

I gave her lots of things, but never yet the ultimate fairy tale.

I'll give her that now. I remember her saying I wish you'd just die. I couldn't believe it. She probably couldn't either. Who knows? I was so outraged and wounded that she would say that. Now I have surrendered. It's fascinating. It's no longer such a big deal. Maybe I'll have a few moments before I go to relish the thing she will say about me to her friends, on Facebook, etc. How I was the love of her life, and how she will never forget me.

Truth is, she won't forget me. She'll be a beautiful widow. I doubt she'll be alone for long. It doesn't matter anymore. In fact, right here, right now, I relish her love for me from after I am gone. The tenderness.

The insurance is in good order, by the way.

I got my second diagnosis yesterday, or second opinion, or whatever you want to call it. The cancer is incurable, spread way too far. So that was the odd pain I've had lately. I didn't know what it was. Now it's spread too far. Just as well. I'm too tired to fight anymore.

We'll both have our fairy tale now. She'll never leave me.

And I do love her. What else can I do?

IN HER DREAMS

In her dreams a man and a woman walk hand in hand, hibiscus or bougainvillea somewhere in the vicinity, like teenagers at the first mystery of reacting to one another's presence. How breathtaking the other one is, like the sea, like the salt wind, like the sun. She tries to save this into waking. She tries to believe one heart can change the world.

An old black man limps into the front of the shuttle bus on crutches. He has a kind face. She jumps up from her seat and smiles at him. "Sit down, please," she says. "No thank you," he replies, looking into her young gray eyes. "But if you want to do something useful, give me a blow job." Her gray eyes widen. She moves to the back of the shuttle as he mumbles something about "useful" once more. She neither cries, nor can she shake this. She doesn't believe he meant any harm, though he did smirk in the end. Being a man, perhaps he cannot feel. She does.

In her dreams she is loyal to the fairy tales that a lovely girl or woman can be loved by everyone in the land, just for her beauty and her kindness, and that men and women would want to bring her gifts.

A fellow student from Greek philosophy, her best friend's fiancé, has fixed her ancient computer once before. This time he brings her an old laptop. "I happened to have this in my parent's garage," he says. "It works good." "Terrific. How much do you want for it?" "It's a gift," he says and grins. "Nobody's using it." "Wow," she says and hugs him after he installs everything she needs. "Can I at least pay you something for your time?" "No," he says, and adds, "You're so beautiful."

"I'm out on limb here," he writes in his email, "but I want to tell you I think you are amazingly sexy. I imagine you naked, with your eyes looking longingly into the distance."

"How to get off the limb," she writes back bravely, "is, you slowly back up toward the trunk and then climb down."

It takes her six weeks to return the laptop because he's always unexpectedly busy and breaks their coffee dates and doesn't show up for class anymore.

He writes her chatty emails from time to time, including telling her how much he eventually got for the old laptop on eBay, including several times asking why she isn't writing back. Finally she does write back: "Because I'm uncomfortable writing to you. Have a beautiful life." She doesn't tell him how afraid she is of his casually entitled presence in her life while he is planning to marry her best friend.

In her dreams, Sheherazade's king doesn't fuck and kill dozens of virgins first before the clever Sheherazade hooks him on her stories and her own brand of sexual surrender, which includes her little sister in the room, first as story prompter and later as a somewhat superfluous witness to all the rest.

Her boyfriend comes carrying luscious red roses, strawberries, and a bottle of Chianti to celebrate the completion of mid-term exams. "Wow, strawberries," she exclaims. Later they lie side by side. She inhales his beautiful skin as he caresses hers. "Would you close your eyes," he asks gently, "and let me come all over your face?" She wants to make him feel good. That's what it's all about, isn't it? But she can't help wondering why. Why this?

Her poetry professor doesn't like what she is writing. "It's cynical," he says. With all her youth and talent, he would prefer her to be starry-eyed. She, too, would prefer to be starry-eyed.

In her dreams she is walking on the beach with her boyfriend, plumeria blossoms tucked behind her ear, a string of shells hanging around his neck. She is looking into his soft dark eyes as the wind blows back his chin-length brown hair. He puts his arms around her shoulder as the sun is gliding down toward the water.

Out in the world, though . . . .

WEDLOCK

Amen, amen! But come what sorrow can . . . .

Romeo

"Makes you look like a blue tulip." John eyed Marian's silky top. This was the first thing he ever said to her.

And so it did, blue blousy material over slim green leggings and light brown ballet flats. Marian was to remember those words for a long time, especially in springtime when the real tulips came out.

"There are no blue tulips," she replied and immediately hoped her voice hadn't been too sharp. She pursed her lips. She couldn't even tell if it was meant as a compliment. She took her head from the French boy's shoulder, smoothed her left hand over her short dark curls, and sat up straight on the maroon corduroy sofa. Someone strummed a guitar nearby.

Michel, the French boy, opened his soft brown-golden eyes, which looked as though they were begging for something, if only for some sort of explanation. She moved an inch away from Michel. Then another. Her cheeks were flushed. She didn't want to do anything to hurt Michel who was nice to her and who had already invited her to come to France, maybe during next spring break. He didn't live too far away from Paris, and she was sure her parents would let her go.

And now there was John, with gray blue eyes, cold like a winter sky, though he was smiling. John was blond, thin, and quite tall, with a bony chiseled face and a narrow nose with flared nostrils. His small-shouldered torso was straight, almost stiff. He had authority.

Later, getting ready for dinner in her dorm room, she was dismayed that she looked so much like a child. Too young. She painted on some black eyeliner, but that only made her look arrogant, not older. She'd never been good at makeup. Nobody had shown her such things, and sometimes she despaired of ever getting it right. It was complicated and always took so much more time than she wanted to give it. She wiped off the stark eyeliner, then masked the resulting pink skin, still smudged, with a thick layer of light-blue iridescent eye shadow. There. On the whole it seemed hopeless, though. She always looked too young without makeup, and then too weird with it.

At the dinner table, John sat down next to Marian, having traded places with one of the youth camp counselors who had sat there for the previous three meals. Michel, who used to sit on Marian's other side, had left that place empty, having been coaxed away, with her blessings solicited and given, by a few girls who found him as charming, it appeared, as Marian had found him at first. His French accent was adorable, his voice was husky to boot, and his manners were impeccable. He was sweet, though he did not seem overly brilliant. But then again, he really had to be quite intelligent, otherwise what was he doing here in the States as an exchange student? He simply got tiresome at times with being so perfectly nice.

At the moment, though, Marian hardly had time to think about such things, for here was John sitting next to her regaling her with, among other things, the Lord's Prayer in Old English, which she thought was absolutely fascinating. He promised to teach it to her, for at the moment she knew it in Latin only, which he apparently knew as well.

It turned out they were both children of church men.

"PKs," John said. "Preacher's kids." She hadn't heard that term before.

"Could be PS, too," she said. "Preacher's spawn." She liked that even better.

John's father, it turned out, had the double distinction of being both a lay minister evangelist and a TV personality. She wasn't personally familiar with him, however, because her own father spurned everybody who wasn't strictly Methodist, which was perhaps not entirely Christian of him, but that's how it was.

Usually Marian was quick to introduce to anyone who would listen, especially boys, the topic of her never wanting to get married. She couldn't remember when she had first said it to anyone. It had to have been three years ago at least, when she was thirteen, and maybe even earlier. She also couldn't remember why exactly she told everybody and his brother. But for one thing, she did mean it, and for another thing, saying it always got attention, especially when she voiced it on dates with boys. It stumped them.

No, marriage wasn't for the likes of her. She wanted to live life. She didn't want to end up like her mother, pleasant, pious, and lifeless. She didn't know yet exactly what she wanted instead, but for now, knowing what she didn't want was enough. For some reason, though—and this was a first in a very long time—she failed to mention this to John. Well, he did talk a lot, and there wasn't much of a chance to get a word in edgewise unless he particularly solicited a response from her. Besides, this wasn't exactly a date. They were, her father's Methodist prejudices notwithstanding, at an ecumenical youth conference where discussing one's relationship preferences was perhaps not the most pressing thing on the agenda. Though, come to think of it, there were official discussions about being gay and Christian. But that was different.

She did manage to tell John that she couldn't possibly study theology, as John said he might consider doing. As far as she was concerned, she knew her father wouldn't care for competition from her, especially with her being a girl.

While they ate side by side and John held forth on various intellectual and spiritual matters, a number of kids stopped by to say hello to her, mostly guys at that, and she basked in the glory of being popular. John, however, didn't seem to notice, which was a pity. She would have liked for him to have noticed. That would have felt like an unspoken answer to some kind of challenge he seemed to emanate, though no challenging words had ever been spoken.

Eventually everybody else had left the dinner table, and only the two of them were still sitting there, when Michel stopped by. "Some of us go dancing," he said. "I'd like the honor if you come with me."

"Oh, I'm a little tired," Marian said. "Go dance. Have fun. I'll just head on up to my room, I think." Parts of her would have loved to go dancing. She glanced at John. He didn't seem interested in dancing.

"Okay," said Michel. He reached for her hand and almost kissed it, then changed his mind and dropped on one knee by her chair and kissed her cheek. "Take good care of yourself."

"You're sweet," she said and stood up to give him a hug, then waved as he left. He looked back over his shoulder once with a twinkle in his golden-brown eyes.

"Well, I'm going up then," she said to John.

"I can meet you at the rose garden in about twenty minutes," he said. "Nobody needs to know."

They did meet at the rose garden that night and held hands for a long time. She wanted to tell him that she didn't normally hold hands that quickly with anyone, but then decided against it. He might not have believed her. And she wasn't quite sure if it was technically true, as she had sometimes held hands with a boy rather suddenly, although not often.

During Christmas vacation, he came to visit her and stayed in the guest bedroom. Marian's mother was the perfect hostess, and her father was aloof as far as she and the proximity of a boy was concerned, while at the same time managing to forge a bond with this budding young theologian, for John had now declared his definite plans for following his own father's footsteps, but properly, with seminary training and all the accoutrements.

Michel had returned to France and they had stopped writing to each other already. Marian didn't even have time to miss Michel, for John was laying claim to her heart and attention, all of which turned out to be time consuming.

John surprised her with a DVD of the old Zefirelli movie *Romeo and Juliet* for a Christmas present, which she had once mentioned in passing as a favorite classic, and which was especially sweet considering that he was a boy, a young man, really, and his ilk usually didn't care for that sort of thing. Even *Moulin Rouge* was sometimes too sappy for young males.

Marian's father officiated at the biggest church in town—physically the biggest, that is. The Lutherans might have had a larger membership, and even the Episcopalians had quite a respectable number in the congregation. There were not many Roman Catholics in town. The day before he left, a Thursday, John asked Marian to visit her father's church with him once more to admire its great beauty. Despite the risk of theft, its doors were always left open, even during the week, so that people could come to find comfort in God's presence.

Somehow everything happened too quickly. Marian had no chance to protest, and didn't know if she wanted to protest in the first place, when John said to her, "I am now marrying you here. Before God. This is our wedding ceremony."

"I'm not sure I want this," she said. Her chest felt constricted. There was an overpowering scent of freesia, vanilla, and wax in the air.

"But you do," he said. "It's fate. Now you are my wife." His smile was firm. His gray blue eyes sparkled.

In some ways it was nice to have someone be decisive like that. After all, he was a year older than she was. She had to trust him now. Anyway, no matter what her views had been before, now it was done.

He took her face in his two hands, kissed her on the forehead, and repeated, "Now you are my wife. My secret wife."

In January, John called her daily, usually late in the evening, and they spoke for hours. Her school work suffered a little, but not too much. A few Bs instead of As. Uncharacteristically for her, this suddenly didn't matter all that much. In February, he called her once or twice a week. The tulips coming out hurt that year. By the time spring break came around, he called maybe once in ten days, although he did email and text more often than that. He had plans for going camping with some friends for spring break.

"What kind of friends?" she wanted to know.

"Just friends," he said.

"Then when will I see you again?" she asked, hating the pleading quality in her own voice.

"Oh, summer, I suppose," he said.

After that he didn't call for three weeks. His emails and texts were nice, but short and far too impersonal for her taste. So she decided to call him. He'd been simply too busy to call or write more elaborately, he said. Besides, you could never trust your privacy with written stuff. He wouldn't want the whole world to have access to what he meant for her eyes only.

This is what she wanted to say to him: Why did you do it? Why did you bind me to you in this secret marriage of yours? I didn't want to be married. And I'm not really married. I know that. You can't just go and say, now we're married. You don't have that kind of authority. But somehow you claimed me, and in my heart I gave you that authority. And now you treat me like I'm a nuisance, and I don't know what to do.

This is what she actually did say to him: "I want to come visit you. Next weekend, for example."

There was a long pause on his end. "Next weekend isn't so good," he eventually said. "Why not wait till summer?"

"No," she said. "I'll come the weekend after next, then."

"Suit yourself," he said.

"Can I stay with you and your folks?" she asked.

"Not a good idea," he said. "I'll find you a place where you can crash."

Her heart sank. Don't you remember that you married me? She wanted to accuse. And that you stayed with my folks? Are you afraid I'll cause a scandal? Drag your name through the mud? Your preciously famous father's name? Instead she said, "Okay."

John found her a place with his good friend, maybe best friend. Bryon was in his second year at seminary and lived in a group house where miscellaneous visitors like herself often got temporary shelter.

Bryon was the one who picked her up at the airport. He was kind. "John couldn't make it," he said. "You must be Marian. He showed me a photo."

She felt a flash of surprising attraction to this good-looking young man. By the time they had completed their ride from the airport to the house where he lived, she was completely comfortable with Bryon. He told her he knew the somewhat younger John because John had applied to the same seminary he currently attended.

Bryon did not put the make on Marian, which was disappointing and reassuring all at the same time. Probably out of friendship for John, of course, but who knew, maybe she had lost some of her allure already over these stressful last six months. At any rate, she was spared the trouble of dodging disquieting advances.

Bryon had a small emblem hanging from the rear view mirror, a red lion on a white crest. Bryon was handsome, thick wavy chestnut brown hair bounced down to his shoulders. He had a full beard and dark brown eyes that glistened with kindness. Under ordinary circumstances she might have fallen in love with him, she thought. But these were no ordinary circumstances.

"We eat at six p.m.," Bryon said.

"Okay. Will John be there?"

"I don't know."

"I have a question," she said. "It's a dumb question, you know. Well, I know at any rate. But I have to ask anyway."

"Ask away."

"Does he have a girlfriend?"

"Not a dumb question," Bryon reassured her. "And, negative. He doesn't. He dates girls from time to time of course. But no girlfriend as such."

You see, I thought I was his girlfriend, Marian wanted to say. Never mind his wife. But that wasn't the kind of thing she could say to someone like John's buddy. I don't want to grovel, and I don't want to be a nuisance. I just want to know where I stand, Marian thought. I want my freedom. I don't understand it, but somehow he took my freedom away.

Bryon showed her the room she would stay in.

"Nice," she said. It had lots of polished trophies, mostly track and field. The room smelled of paper, dust, and a little bit of sweat.

"It belongs to a guy named Martin," Bryon said. "He's gone for the weekend. He said to tell you, pardon his Bibles."

"He's a seminary student, too?" Marian asked.

"Yes. We all are, the permanent residents here. So, the bathroom is down that way." Bryon pointed down the blue carpeted hall. "And do have supper with us. There will be at least one other girl, probably two. And if you want to use the phone to call John, it's in the living room."

"Thanks," Marian said. "I got my cell phone, though."

I really only want to know what's going on, she told herself.

John was not there when supper started, so she sat down with Bryon and a boy named Carl and a girl named Nikki. She ate quietly, smiled politely when it seemed to be called for, said a few words now and again. Please. Thank you. No, I'm just a senior in high school. That sort of thing.

John came when supper was almost over. He came with a girl.

"Kate, Marian. Marian, Kate," he introduced. "I had to give Kate here a ride," he said as though by way of apology for being late. "Good to see you, Marian." He did not, however, look particularly pleased.

Kate seemed to not be his girlfriend, or if so, she had been warned not to act too possessively. Kate hugged Bryon and snuggled with him on the sofa for a bit, but even that seemed to be just camaraderie, no sizzling chemistry. But then neither was there any noticeable chemistry between herself and John, though they were, and then again were not, husband and wife.

Secretly married. Forever. Though it was mostly invisible. No welts. No scars. Or would others notice over time how she lugged shame with her like a dreadful gilded chain?

"So what's up?" John asked. She engaged in a short while of small talk. My parents say to say hello, and so on.

Fairly soon, she didn't know what to do, so finally she got up to go to her room. Once there, she knew she should have said, Oh, John, come. I want to show you something I brought for you. But she hadn't been able to think of that ruse in time to make use of it.

However, John did knock on her door after a few minutes. Relieved, she asked him in. He left the door a crack open.

"So here you are," he said, looking at her with sparkling crystal clear eyes. Was there fear in his eyes as well?

"Yes," she said. She wanted to ask him, Why did you pretend to marry me when you didn't mean it? You changed my whole life, and now I feel like a prisoner in my own skin. Instead, she asked the most courageous question she could muster. "Why do you never call anymore?"

Another thing she wanted to ask, but didn't, was, What do you want from me?

Nothing, he seemed to want to answer to that question. I just want you to go away. Go away please. Okay?

Well, she wanted to say, I've done everything that a married woman does. I've loved you. I've cried for you. I've gone for walks with you, both real and imaginary. But there's one thing that married people do that we haven't done.

She went to the door and closed it all the way and locked it. She had checked earlier that there was a lock on the door and how to work it. She didn't say anything, but silently got undressed, folding her garments meticulously, tucking her white underwear underneath.

"What do you want me to do?" he asked.

She smiled crookedly and looked into his eyes. "What do you think?"

He looked concerned and uneasy, but started taking off his clothes as well.

"I don't want you to get pregnant," he said. "So I'm going to have to pull out early. Okay?"

She nodded.

She was afraid. And angry. Infinitely sad. This is not how things were supposed to be. And they were of course not married, and she knew it. But she also knew that she was not free of him until . . . actually she didn't know what exactly would have to happen for her to be free again, to live, to look forward to life. This sex thing? She was doing it to spite him, to slap his face for what he had done to her, for what he had stolen from her. She knew he couldn't possibly understand what she was doing. In all likelihood, she'd just be a notch on his belt or something like that. For her, it was a bit like committing suicide in order to prevent someone else from coming along to kill her, that sort of thing.

She felt physical stirring in her pelvis, a mild heat. She knew she was losing him, had lost him already. She wanted to get it over with. So many realities all at once. The real thing. A girl's last trump. But for her it wasn't a trump, it was a reckless act of defiance. Is this what you wanted?

He thrust into her. It was a burning sensation, as there had been no anticipatory wetness, though he took some spittle to wet the entrance to her body, but it wasn't much. Then there was a small sharp sensation inside her, a peculiar pull of nerves that she had never felt before, like a taut string snapping against tender skin and filling out into an elongated ache. That was that. No more virginity. She felt a mixture of anger and sadness wound up tightly in her chest.

He was on top of her and thrust only six times before he pulled himself out and shortly thereafter ejaculated on top of her soft belly.

That was it, then? she thought. Other thoughts in her mind were, Why? Why is this so important? Any of it, and all of it?

She hadn't realized there would be liquid on top of her, so she reached over and grabbed her top, the same blue tulip blouse she had worn at camp last summer, and she started wiping off the liquid on her belly, then her crotch. There were a few drops of blood. Not much. Then she offered the blouse to him.

"Thanks," he said and wiped his penis before putting on his light gray cotton underpants. He had a pale-skinned washboard abdomen.

She got up, moving slowly like a dancer, rummaged in her suitcase, found a clean top and pulled it over her head.

For some time they sat opposite each other, she in yoga position, he squatting over his heels. He looked angry. She in turn *was* angry. Also puzzled. Confused. Aching with shame and loss.

"I guess you better go now," she said.

She wanted to ask him so many questions. She wanted to accuse him, too. She wanted to cry. She also wanted to accuse, not just him, but everybody else who had contributed so little to her life so that she now didn't know what to do.

"Okay," he said, stood up, unlocked the door and left the room, closing the door softly behind him again.

She heard his footsteps tap along the muffling hallway carpet. Footsteps muffled in blue.

She didn't want to see anyone and tiptoed to the bathroom when she was sure that there would be no one in the hallway. She washed herself, not using any of the towels or washcloths there, just using her hands.

Back in her room she cried herself to sleep.

The next morning she woke early and met Bryon in the kitchen.

"Coffee?" he asked.

"Yes, please," she said. "Do you have time to take me to the airport?"

"Of course," he said. "But you're welcome to stay longer. Stay as long as you like."

"Thanks," she said. "I don't think . . . ." She wanted to explain. She also wanted to build a wall of silence around her.

"I understand. Nonrefundable tickets and all that," Bryon said.

Of course he understood nothing at all. However, he was kind. He stopped to get gas on the way to the airport and presented her with a miniature plush blue teddy bear from the convenience store. HUGS, it said on a heart-shaped tiny placard. She laughed.

"What's the joke?" Bryon asked.

"I like it," she said. "A teddy bear. Not a Bible."

He rolled his eyes at her.

Though Bryon sent her a Christmas card the following winter, and one more the winter after that, Marian never heard from John again. For a while, when her cell phone rang, she felt an electricity of hope or apprehension, some sharp nerve jolt related to John. After a while that peculiar response went away.

Sometimes she thought of Michel, whom she imagined happy, dancing somewhere near Paris with an elegant sweetheart. She wished him well, the sweet boy whom she had thrown over just to be secretly married and tied forever by an invisible thread to a heaviness that could, like so many other things, never be expressed. For it was a life in which no one ever had the courage or the kindness to ask, "What's wrong?"

MEADOW GIRL

It was summer. I sat by wild roses just in bloom. The ocean before me, delicious sun above, the fragrance of recently cut grass. Tiny white daisies that had bent to escape the mower already stood up again triumphantly. Near me to the left were a mother with two children on a picnic blanket, a boy and a slightly bigger girl, both golden-haired in the sunlight, though the mother's hair was dark and fashionably cut chin-length and layered in back.

The girl hummed a song. Her braids were loosened by the breeze. She had picked a handful of daisies and held them out to her mother. "For you."

"Later," her mother said briskly, busy with packing up their picnic supplies.

Suddenly a skirmish, ending in a reprimand and an indignant defense.

"Mom, I was just sitting there. Tommy poked me with his picnic fork. Twice."

"Well, I didn't see it."

"Because your back was turned."

"Both times?"

"Yes, both times."

"Well, he's only five. He doesn't know what he is doing."

"He does so know."

The boy reached for his mother's hand. She took it. His eyes were round and blue and pleading.

"Mom, my arm hurts where he poked me."

"I don't want to hear about this anymore."

"You're listening to him."

"He hasn't said a word."

"He's holding your hand. That counts."

"And it tells me what a good little boy he is."

"But listen to me, too. Please, Mom."

"I've heard enough."

"No, you haven't."

"Of course I have."

There was one more thing the girl could do. The piercing scream. Even the roar of the water was not loud enough to drown it out.

"That's enough out of you, Missy. Come, Tommy. We'll go and leave her here until she is done screaming and being a bad girl."

Tommy shot his sister a proud look. Her screams swelled. She threw herself on the ground. Perhaps this had worked for her in the past. Today it didn't work. Today Tommy won.

Hand in hand, the mother and small son were already halfway up the meadow on the slope of the hill leading up to trees and houses on the right. They were almost to the top of the hill when the girl stood up, her face pink, her light blue dress darkened with grass stains. If they turned the corner onto the path among the trees, she would lose sight of them.

"Wait," she shouted and stumbled after them.
I picked up the small bunch of daisies she left behind.

A MOMENT AT THE WINDOW

Her fingers hold the white curtains and the light blue drapes. Her hand is steady. Her heart is not.

Wren has never worn a hat. His greetings are done with a flourish of his left hand. He knows how to project. Still. Or again, as the case may be. The little girl Lily, three houses down, runs to greet him, then struggles with frustration at the white fence in her way. He simply lifts her over the fence. For a moment, Marialena at the curtain holds her breath. Is it wise? But the lift of the now beaming four-year-old proceeds without incident.

His given name is Lionel. Everyone calls him Wren. Nobody remembers how that started, not even Wren himself. Or so he says. Nel wouldn't have worked. Neither would Ly.

Moments later, Lily has been deposited back behind her fence, waving frantically as Wren continues down the street. His step is brisk, with a small swagger. His hair is almost all silver now, but at least he still has a full head of it. The girl's mother, Maggie, waves at him too now from the porch. For a moment, all poised to drop the curtain, Marialena thinks he might look back at the house. But no, he struts along and she keeps the narrow triangle of vision open.

His flamboyance makes her smile. But high up in her chest she also feels an ache. For him. And for herself. Leaves float to the sidewalk. Wren kicks a pile of raked ones. So beautiful. His steps. The gardens. The fences. Late roses blooming on his left. His disposition is sunny, as it has always been. Or almost always. She knows he is meeting his lover. His mistress. Whatever it's called these days. Or, rather, she doesn't exactly know. He has always done her the honor of making his associations most vague, both before and after his heart attack.

Before he used to meet up with one of his women friends for alleged tennis matches, from which he typically returned smelling much cleaner than he when had left. Well, it stood to reason, didn't it? You'd shower after a tennis match rather than right before. Nowadays he goes for long recuperative walks. They aren't certain yet whether he will ever be able to play tennis again. At this point the main concern is still what he can and cannot eat to keep his arteries unclogged. Kyla, an astonishingly young woman also in recovery, whom Marialena has met just once, is a member of his support group and has eagerly agreed to be his daily walking buddy. The rest remains unspoken. But Marialena knows. He leaves for these walks wearing the same aftershave with which he also returns. Does he keep a bottle at Kyla's house? He has always been considerate and respectful.

She remembers how in the past, at times like this, she used to dance in the master bedroom. In front of the full length mirror, any mirror, really, she always danced better and far more wildly than in public. You could only ever really sparkle in private. Out on a public dance floor, there was often either not enough space for a sweeping waltz, which Wren had finally mastered after many years of marriage, or else she had to tone down her Cuban motion and body ripples when they went to an occasional salsa club, so as to not out-dance him. It always felt as though arrows of judgment would come hissing her way if she were to step out of line and steal more than her fair share of the show. Oh, she'd been a splendid dancer, even in full view of the constricting public. Now, however, her varicose veins are bothering her too much to even flirt privately with herself at length in the mirror.

It should have been a splendid life. Her mind flits to their wedding. The photographer's blinding flash. The dinner in the church basement with a borrowed disco ball overhead. Her sparkling dress, her veil, held with rhinestone pins in her thick brown hair. Wren's intense dark eyes softening every time he looked at her while bantering with their guests. How he stumbled three times in their simple wedding waltz after he'd had only two lessons at the time, but it didn't matter because of his eyes. The awkward excitement of the wedding night. She was a virgin. No telling what he was, but he was gentle and beside himself with enthusiasm.

She loves him with anger and with gentleness. She wishes him happy. There is so little time in life to begin with, even without the menace of fragile health. But where did his desire go? And why? God was playing a terrible prank, designing men one way and women another.

Wren knows fidelity and exclusivity are important to her. She knows his unbridled sexuality is stronger than his innocent wish to keep her happy and unharmed. There is no knowing how much time he has left, and she loves him. She doesn't want to be his prison. She doesn't even want to be a fence.

Down the street he is approaching the corner where he always turns left. Just before he turns, a shaft of sunbeam breaks through the clouds, like a spotlight softening the air around his shimmering shape.

His happiness or hers. It isn't really a choice. He does what he does. She does what she does. She chooses to fence in her own needs so that his can roam freely. It isn't easy. Bridled rage spills inside her. How long will the punctured veneer of love safely contain it?

She drops the curtain and the drape and reclines on the sofa with another romance novel where the hero, created by a woman writer of course, is so stunned by a personal connection that he can easily give up any and all dreams of other women. A tear slides down her face. The Duke of So-And-So chooses to be forever faithful to his bride after a sumptuous sex scene which Marialena has skimmed. These lusty scenes seem to be *de rigeur* these days. She could do without, but she has already read all of Georgette Heyer and other writers of sexless tales, most of them several times over.

Once she had dreams that she was exceptional, like the soon to be new Duchess of So-and-So, in whose case the usual laws of reality do not apply. Exceptional. The laws of male nature do not apply. Lovely. Her tears flow freely now. She is content with that. She has to be content.

Once, too, she dreamt that when a woman was sad and shared her sadness with a man she loved, then he would love her in return and do all in his power to protect her fragile beauty and vulnerability. She found it isn't so.

Her eyelids feel heavy. In a few moments she will fall asleep. The book will slide out of her hands and down into the thick carpet. When he returns, smelling of aftershave and blameless hand soap, he will tuck the soft blanket around her shoulders. Perhaps he will stop for a moment to look at her

face. Then he will proceed to the kitchen and cook up a
healthy supper for the two of them.

A PAINTING INSIDE A PAINTING

"You don't have those lines quite right," the teacher said.

She was right. My sculpture was sleek and slender. The model was fat. Her face was exquisite, though, except for that brief instant when she took off her robe—at that moment her face was silly, distorted in an apologetic grin. Then afterwards her face was meditative and beautiful again. I thought I could see worlds in her eyes, spinning in sunlit anonymity. But we weren't allowed to do faces yet, only the body; and I had begun to love my sculpture, slender and all wrong, reddish brown clay hugging its armature, just as the model herself was pensively hugging her knees for $8.00 an hour, which was way over minimum wage in those days, but not exactly enormous wealth.

Suddenly I disliked my teacher. I studied her own sculptures—many of them were on display—with critical eyes. Her St. Francis with three birds on his left arm was stumpy and looked neither particularly serene nor benign. Her Romeo and Juliet stood awkward and furtive on their balcony suggested by three bars of railing. The teacher's own face was covered with the spider webs of age, and the lines hugging her mouth looked bitter with failure. Here she was teaching adult rank beginners at her home studio on Raven Street, rather than being feted in New York or Chicago.

Meanwhile I was incomprehensibly hurt. I wasn't here to learn to be a sculptor anyway, I had to remind myself. I wanted to write about a sculptor, not become one. I merely needed to learn the rudiments of some foreign craft.

I amended my clay to my teacher's satisfaction, fattening the lines. I wasn't half bad at following directions. But I never liked my sculpture again. I've often thought I should have just dropped out of class with my sculpture while I was still in love with it. But I didn't. I was so afraid I would miss something if I didn't follow my teacher's directions.

I did grow to like the teacher again a little for taking us on a field trip to a lost wax foundry in Albuquerque and we happened to get there just as hot metal was poured. I was spellbound. I did not, however, take my own sculpture to be made into a bronze. Of course not, as I never liked it again. Nor did I ever venture to make another. The clay, armature, and two small carving tools all ended up on a giveaway table in the Laundromat one year after spring cleaning.

The years rolled by, day after day, towards sunrise. I hardly noticed, though I witnessed a thousand ways of the world. Photographers worried more about exposure and light than the dreams of their subjects. True, one could argue some of their subjects, shipyard chain links and church steeples, never dreamed in the first place. All that mattered were textbook textures and robust geometry and the docile homage to reality. Reality itself of course was always slanted with the quest for respect and applause. An ever-critical intellect was highly valued, as was the classical and sometimes crass delivery of cynicism.

Meanwhile my soul was brimming with rejected unicorns and princesses, puffy-eyed with weeping, some dragging behind them soggy robes through bogs of moldy innocence. And so I limped along with fuzzy longing and sometimes I got drunk with disappointment.

But then once upon a time I limped into a respectable museum in a gray polluted city by the sea. There were the usual pamphlets and upturned noses of discernment, when suddenly I saw a painting of an artist painting the portrait of a woman. The dominant colors were muted brown and beige. The model in the painting was stern. Her mouth was tight with bored entitlement. Two children on either side of her looked stiff and brave. Meanwhile the woman on the easel in the painting inside the painting was lovely with soft features, and the children were leaning towards her. That day I fell in love with life again.

I went to see the painting three more times, each time staying as long as reality permitted. Then I had to leave the city to come home. Now, though, I knew the way.

Part III:

Fairy tales

ON THE SIDE OF THE MOUNTAIN

She sat on the side of the mountain, asters and marigolds dancing their celebration of late summer in soft wind. Dragonflies and grasshoppers with bright red wings lit up the grass. Rain had been plentiful and everything was lush.

Next to her in the grass, the prince: his hair dark and splendid, his skin lined with a story of much play in the sun. His head rested on top of his two hands. His right leg was bent over the top of his left. He had a blade of grass in his mouth and his eyes were closed. He was dreaming, probably of being an eagle.

She kept her own eyes wide open. There were venomous critters in this land and she dreaded being stung or bitten in the middle of a dream. A horned lizard zigzagged into the open palm of her hand, making her smile.

What do you have to tell me, my friend?

Only that the world is beautiful, though dangerous, too.

A tear fell on the lizard's skin, for in her heart it was winter, her love all covered with snow. She envied his ability to sleep and dream while she must worry about scorpions and rattlesnakes and other dangers, though none were likely to materialize.

Yes, it was winter in her heart, and the snow kept falling.

He's not that into you, said the voice of her heart snow.

He has given me my own room in his castle and a tree in his garden, she argued in his defense.

Yes, but if an avalanche came down the mountain side and threatened to bury you both, would you stay with him?

Of course I would.

And if he broke his leg and couldn't move, and it looked like you wouldn't be found for days, would you still stay with him?

Of course. I would find herbs under the snow. I would even kill a rabbit.

And would he stay with you if you broke a bone?

At this question some of the ice around her heart began to melt with treacherous love for herself. The horned lizard jumped out of her hand. Goodbye. She imagined her leg broken, the dark settling in, and the cold settling in, the sun going down in the west. Gold light still in the sky.

Would he stay?

At first he would be drawn to her. She would not beg, of course, no heartfelt "don't go" from her lips. Soon she would encourage him to go. No point in both of them tempting death when one of them could easily survive.

But would you like him to stay?

Yes, of course.

But he will not?

No. Probably not.

You should go, she'd tell him, never mind her true desires. Go save yourself.

What about you?

Clearly I can't go anywhere.

I'll send help, my love, he'd say.

It wouldn't come in time she knew, but didn't say. Soon any pain would be over anyway, giving way to blessed endorphins flooding her growing distance from life.

I shouldn't leave you here, he'd say.

But he would. She knew it. Yes, you should go, she'd say. No point in both of us being stuck here in the maw of difficulty.

Of course if she were staying with him, he would thank her for her presence as she wrapped herself around him against the cold. She loved life, but from the first she knew she would be willing to give it up for him.

But he was different. Go, she would tell him. Just go.

And then the image of him sauntering down the side of the ice-covered mountain, so happy for his chance to keep on living.

So much for winter in her heart. She had to climb through it on her own, and she knew she could make it, even if she had to crawl on her knees.

She looked at him, still lying in the summer grass. He opened his brown summer eyes.

"What a beautiful day," he sighed in breathy summer voice.

"Yes, beautiful," she said and moved closer through all the ice and the snow.

THE LITTLE MERMAID: A FEW MOMENTS WITH THE QUEEN

I don't want to be ungrateful here, with my grandchildren at my feet and all that. But sometimes I wish I were that mystical and insubstantial creature that dissolved from love struck mermaid first into foam, then air. Sometimes I wish I, too, would be remembered not for what is or was, but for what could have been. If only.

Happy? Let's say I am content. And not entirely content to be content. I'd love to have ended up happy. But that would have required my husband's commitment. And I'm not so sure he's capable of all out commitment. The physical aspect is okay. He appreciates his Sunday roasts, his wine, his massages, his sex. He will not leave me.

I'm talking human dilemma here. Testosterone. Estrogen. And the incompatible dreams.

I've been married to the erstwhile prince for twenty-five years now. I know my man. I know his aches, his moods, his foibles. Just as he all too frequently reminds me of mine.

You see, he always loves best what is just out of reach. Perhaps we all do. Although I have loved one fierce reality. There was a boy, not my prince, who touched the inside of my elbow once, and I was so stunned by the exquisite pleasure that I replay that touch today in memory when I need comfort in this bread and butter world.

When the little mermaid, my prince's pet girl, his mute foundling, slept on his doorstep every night, then he dreamt of me. Then I was the mysterious girl from the monastery who found him on the beach. He pretended that he did not wake up until I came along, and he pretended that I rescued him. Then he pretended it was fate, ordained by god, etc. It was convenient, since it turned out that our parents wanted us to make a political alliance by marriage in the first place.

Meanwhile he had her sleep on his door step, telling her she was his favorite of all. To a point.

Now he is getting older, but still imposing. A little slower with everything, that's all. He has his daily massages and flirts with the servants. He is convinced he is charming, using the same phrases and benevolently raised eyebrows his father used before him. Using the same phrases, in fact, that my own elderly father uses. Go figure.

Thing is, my prince never really wanted to do much of anything. He didn't come courting me. He didn't come doing anything at all. There was no dragon. No difficulty whatsoever.

And who does he now dream of? The one who was willful and sentimental, totally unrealistic, cost everybody a great deal, most of all herself at that. Her love for my husband cost her her own most precious voice. Isn't that often the case for a woman, human or merfolk?

As for me, the older I get, the more I learn. I'm not even fifty years old yet, and already a grandmother. Soon the grandkids will ask me for fairy tales, and tales of how our family came to be, tales of how we met one day by the sea. Will I tell them the dreams of happily ever after? So that they will be comforted in their gullible youth that it will all turn out well one day, and then be bitterly disappointed later on when their prince or princess has feet, not even of clay, but of mere flesh and blood? For the longest time I couldn't grasp that it wasn't all about me, prince, crown, happy ending, marriage, and all. That my so-called happy ending was another's tragedy. And perhaps vice versa.

So I lie in bed reading poems and mystery novels, and he sits on his mahogany rocking chair on the terrace facing the sea, dreaming of her.

I know she flies through the world visiting, especially children, in the shape of the spirit of the air she became. Did she visit our children? Will she now visit our grandchildren and place air kisses on their foreheads, filling their hearts with dazzling dreams of things that we have all wished for and none of us have ever been selfless enough to fulfill?

The sea witch was the only one who didn't lie. Everything has its price, and oftentimes the price is beyond what anyone in their right mind should be willing to pay. Her magical voice. Her sisters' beautiful hair. My peace of mind.

I wish he could have loved me like a fairy tale. Like I, too, once thought it was promised, kissed by God only knows what spirit. The way he loved me at first, when I was still out of reach. Instead . . . .

As I said, I am content, but not happy. That is perhaps the worst that could have happened, this achy kind of gratitude that knows that I'm stuck with what there is, and it is good, but it should have been better, and I only have this one fairy tale, and even in this fairy tale I am bleeding over the borders.

If I were a cat, maybe it would be enough to be content. But I am not a cat.

My heart is not broken, just bruised.

I assume at night he dreams of her and yearns for her—
maybe the air brushes his forehead and he feels kissed by her
spirit self. I remind myself, as though it mattered, that when
she was there, he let her sleep on his doorstep, his little mute
foundling. But now that she is gone, she's ever treasured in
his mind and has assumed cosmic proportions. I'm not
consigned to his doorstep, thank God for that. But I'm
permanently consigned to some sort of anteroom of his
heart, while he's spent the last twenty-five years of reality
building a mystic temple in his heart for her.

He doesn't speak of it; he leaves us that much dignity.
But I can tell he is in love with her. He thinks she is
exquisitely important in her elegant absence.

A man's love always has a price. As does a man's
indifference to reality. His mute foundling lost her voice and
her mermaid life as a price for love. I am paying a price, too,
I'm sure, though I'm not certain what it is.

THE MOST BEAUTIFUL VOICE

"Where are you going?" asked the laughing young king.

"I have to attend the birth of a girl. She'll have the most beautiful voice in all the world one day," said his brown-eyed gypsy lover. "I have to give her a blessing."

"Then I'll come with you," said the king, winding one of her long black curls around his gentle fingers.

After the little girl emerged from between her mother's legs and was presented to her father and the assembled guests, she cried out once, an ordinary baby's cry of considerable anguish. The king looked at the gypsy, the gypsy looked at the king.

"Not yet," she said. "That was just her baby cry."

So enchanted was the king with his sparkling gypsy lover and her interest in this newborn baby that he promised to raise the girl in his castle as though she were his own daughter.

At first the parents stalled. The mother held her small baby close to her chest.

"She'll have a good life with me," the king said. "Much better than here."

The mother's face creased in consternation.

The king noticed three boys hanging back by the door, peering into the room with enormous round eyes.

"I'll also pay to raise your boys," the king said. "I'll give them an education."

That was an offer too good to pass up, at least so the father thought.

"She will have a voice golden like the sun and silver like the moon. Her name will be Chantal," the gypsy whispered to the mother.

And so the king and the gypsy raised the girl who grew and prospered and smiled and played and started singing happy songs. She walked in the king's garden in a shimmering white dress among the roses and the larkspur. Soon she was allowed to eat at the king's table, and sometimes she sang duets with the gypsy. Together they made gorgeous harmonies. The gypsy taught her to coo and to trill, and sounds of joy and praise, and they ate sugar plums and other delicacies.

For seven years Chantal lived with the king and his gypsy love. Then one day, the gypsy died.

The king was inconsolable. He kissed his lover's lifeless brow one last time. The girl, too, bent over her gypsy face and placed a kiss on her cheek.

The king really, really tried. But the little girl reminded him too much of his lost gypsy lover and he could no longer bear her presence.

So one day he had a suitcase packed for her, and a large chest of sweetmeats.

He carried the girl in his own arms to her parent's house, which now looked far less shabby than it had at her birth.

"I've brought you back your daughter to raise," he said.

"When will you come to take me back to where I live?" Chantal asked the king.

"This is where you live now," the king said. And Chantal looked around her and was frightened. "These are your parents," the king added.

The parents were of mixed mind. They had already given her up to what they thought was a fabulous fate. Besides, they didn't even know the girl. But when they learned that the king would not stop their sons' allowance even though now their daughter was back home with them, they resigned themselves to raising the girl.

They didn't dare ask, would the king come back for her when the girl was raised? The king, for his part, didn't feel compelled to volunteer that he wanted the girl off his hands forever.

Chantal was pretty and her voice was beautiful indeed.

When her parents asked her to show them how she had spent her days at the castle, she tried, but they didn't know anything about pleasure gardens and royal tables and chandeliers, and she couldn't show them. Then, too, the roses at the king's garden were much larger than the climbing roses at her mother's kitchen door, though the larkspur growing wild in the corner of the yard behind the dung heap here was the same size as at the castle.

The other thing that was the same was Christmas day when they had roast goose for their dinner. "That's what we ate at the king's table," Chantal said, glad that she could finally tell them about something besides larkspur.

One day her mother discovered that a music teacher lived in the nearby town.

"We could take just a few coins from the boys' allowance each."

"No," said the father. "The boys' allowance is for them. If the king wanted her to have lessons, he would have made provisions."

"Perhaps he didn't think of it?" the mother ventured.

"I said no," said the father. "The boys' allowance is theirs. Besides, she's supposed to have the most beautiful voice in any case. The gypsy said so. Why waste good money, when it's supposed to happen anyway?"

The mother left it at that. She loved watching her daughter in the garden, singing to flowers and squirrels, and even to pigs. But one day, being timid and feeling, too, that perhaps a voice as beautiful as that was more precious than they deserved, the mother thought to herself, what if her marvelous voice broke one day from too much use? What if the beautiful voice were damaged and they would be blamed for it? Besides, it didn't seem right to squander a precious voice on pigs or squirrels or even roses. What if there was a limit to beauty? So she told her daughter not to sing anymore, and not to speak anymore either, so as to protect her precious voice.

The king had not entirely forgotten, but he longed to forget because he wanted to get over the loss of his gypsy lover. He never succeeded. He never found a replacement for his lover, though he looked. He didn't want to be reminded. So he never came back to visit, much less to claim Chantal with her beautiful voice.

Meanwhile, the other children in the village school made fun of silent Chantal who felt she had to obey. Once, just one time, she sang to herself alone in the garden. But her mother had returned from an errand sooner than expected and looked at her with such sorrowful eyes that Chantal never tried it again.

She learned enough at school to write notes to her mother. In one of them she begged to let her stay away from the school where the other children only laughed at her.

For a while she climbed trees and went for walks.

"Don't move too much," her mother said one day. "We don't want to damage your voice in any way."

She learned from books, as is often the case with children who are not allowed to use their voices or to move too much. Her face was pale. She had a cat she liked to pet, but even the cat was often busy with many other things. Sometimes she wasn't quite sure whether she was really awake and really alive.

Her brothers did well. One became a doctor, one became a teacher, one opened a shop with jewels and chinaware. They married and led prosperous and fruitful lives. They visited rarely. But one day one of them came with his boy, already five years old, who liked to examine the world. He discovered a great many things.

"Look, a cat," he cried. "An egg. A lamb!" He especially liked the lamb. "Larkspur," he exclaimed as he ventured near the dung heap.

Even after he was called inside for dinner, he still wasn't finished making discoveries, for at the dinner table, silent and gray with invisibility, was Chantal.

"What is that?" He didn't recognize her as someone human, so still and colorless had she become. This startled everyone. They had mostly forgotten her well-behaved presence.

"Oh, that's your Aunt Chantal."

"Is she human?" he asked.

"Yes."

"Can I touch her?"

"Better not."

"Would she break?"

"Perhaps."

"Why is she like that?"

"Nobody knows. She once lived with a king. Maybe that's why."

"Why did she live with a king?"

"Because she has the most beautiful voice in the world."

"Can I hear it?"

"No. She's saving it."

"For what?"

Pale Chantal stood up in a panic. What would happen if she actually opened her mouth now after all these years? What if, after so much promise, she wasn't good enough?

Her heart felt frozen. Her voice felt frozen.

She remembered the king. She remembered having been put aside, then saved for some nebulous future, fading away like some unused treasure in the attic. She remembered songs she should be singing, trees she should be climbing, hearts she should be touching. She remembered the gypsy most of all, with her love and her freedom and her carefree strength. There was no one like that in Chantal's life now to guide her or love her or even just to notice her. Chantal had been betrayed with a promise of beauty which she was then not allowed to use, just in case.

And so she opened her mouth.

There was the rasp of clearing her throat. Then, like rust crumbling, her scream shattered the stunned silence around her. Even the chickens stopped pecking in the yard. The pain was great, and the long neglected voice expressed it to perfection. Spoons and forks clattering to the table top made the only other sound. The people at the table held their breath, especially the little boy who was frightened and pulled his hands over his ears.

What an ugly voice, everyone thought, pierced by the roar of pain. The mother was afraid it might be heard all the way in town, or, worse, even at the king's castle. It sounded like a beast in agony.

"This is what I know," Chantal said, with bitterness falling from her mouth like flint. "First you gave me a promise, then you abandoned me. You left me to wither. You've never listened to me. Now do you expect me to make beauty with my voice? Or would you rather I kept silent forever about what I know of all the wrong choices, all the mistakes?"

But suddenly her voice changed, and her skin and her eyes took on color.

"And you know what?" she said. "No matter what, I can do that. Now it is time to praise the world." Already she started sounding like a song. "Now it is time to sing of the beauty of things, so that we don't forget again. How beautiful things are when we don't forget what we have. Life. Yes. And whatever befalls us can never change our true nature. Never. Look. Listen. The blackbirds, the geese, the grasses. The chickens back to clucking over their grain. If I sounded like a monster to you, it is because you have kept me silent too long. It is my destiny to be loud, to make you cry for what has been lost to neglect and mistakes, and then to comfort you with what remains. The blazing magic of your life. But before I can give you your own beauty, you have to let me open my mouth."

The little boy stood up, too, now and moved around the table and took her hand. Together they walked away from the table and out into the garden, and beyond it to the town.

When the sun went down that night, the boy stood waving to her from his own parents' house where he stayed behind while she kept on walking, through the town, through the country, past the castle, on into the world, where she sang and sang and sang.

If you are a woman and you listen to the gold and silver in your heart, deep down below the pale obedience, you can hear her even now.

ACKNOWLEDGMENTS

Thank you to the following publications in which these stories previously appeared, some in slightly different form:

52/250. "The Good Guys"

5923 Quarterly. "Sarah," "Wedlock"

Blue Print Review. "In Her Dreams"

Caravel Literary Arts Journal. "The Doll Elizabeth"

Cirque. "The Mistakes"

Constellations: A Journal of Poetry and Fiction. "The Footnote"

Eclectica Magazine. "Annette and Florian"

Eighty Percent. "Eclipse"

Eternal Haunted Summer. "Imagine"

Ghoti. "Colors"

Hot Metal Press. "Sarah"

The Linnet's Wings. "Good Friday – Mary Magdalen"

The Miscreant. "Whore," "I Know"

Moondance. "Good Friday – Mary Magdalen," "Fourteen Days in November"

Mused Bella Online. "Woodcut"

origami journal. "The Girl Who Moved to Atlanta"

Peacock Journal. "A Painting Inside a Painting," "On the Side of the Mountain"

Piker Press: "Strange Justice," "The Demonstration," "Eclipse," "Sarah"

Pure Slush: "Meadow Girl"

River Poets Journal: "Annette and Florian," "A Moment at the Window"

Rose & Thorn Journal: "Strange Justice," "A Moment at the Window"

Salome: "Isis," "The Lucky Children"

Scarlet Leaf Review: "One Year"

Three Drops from a Cauldron: "The Little Mermaid: A Few Moments with the Queen"

Thrice Fiction: "Her Fairy Tale"

Whistling Shade: "The Most Beautiful Voice"

The Write Place at the Write Time: "The Little Mermaid: A Few Moments with the Queen"

Writers' Bloc: "The Demonstration"

About the Author

Beate Sigriddaughter, www.sigriddaughter.net, was poet laureate of Silver City, New Mexico (Land of Enchantment) from 2017 to 2019. Her work has received several poetry awards. Červená Barva Press published her poetry chapbook *Dancing in Santa Fe* and other poems in 2019 and Unsolicited Press published her poetry chapbook *Emily* (February 2020).